D0818760

Other books
by
Terry Howard

The Flying Four
Matthew's Schooldays
Mirror to the Past
The Time Police
The Time Police 2
    - *Draco Returns!*
The Time Police 3
    - *Invasion!*
Bytes
Doors

The Little Book of Proverbs

by

Terry Howard

Contents

For: *L.I.G.*

THE BANK JOB

The Governor of the Bank of England, James Pattison sat in his large office at the uppermost level of the Bank building on Threadneedle Street, London. He was a large man with receding wavy hair and large sidewhiskers, with honest, clear dark eyes, longish nose and pursed lips. He wore a high-necked white shirt, beneath a purple double-breasted short jacket with long coat tails, white breeches to his knees and white stockings with buckled black leather shoes. The office was fitted all round in polished oak panelled walls, with portraits of previous bank governors upon them, and a deep yellow and gold carpet filled the office floor from wall to wall. His extremely large desk was solid polished oak, as was his swivel chair with its deep red leather seat. Four brass lamps with blue glass shades stood on the corners of the desk, with a gold inkstand with a long feathered quill nearby; the desk was unusually clear of any other paperwork. The Governor sat and stared at just one letter, which lay opened on his desk.

There was a discreet tap on his large polished oak office door, which was quite a long way from his desk at the end of the vast room. 'Come in.' Governor Pattison said in no more than a whisper. The door slowly opened and in walked Mister Thomas Newman, Chief Clerk of the bank, a tall man with little hair on his shiny dome of a head, thin eyebrows over sad eyes, long nose and slanted mouth. He wore a similar outfit to the Governor, but his jacket was black, and he carried a large oblong wooden box.

'Good Morning sir... you wished to see me.' Thomas said as he approached the desk.

'Good morning Thomas,' answered the Governor, 'it's about the post.'

'Why, I have it here,' said Thomas, lifting the wooden box towards his employer, 'I always bring it to you, first thing every morning.'

'Then how did this get here?' The Governor pointed at

the only two items on his large desk, a letter and its opened envelope, 'did you bring this letter in earlier this morning?'

'No. Definitely not. The last time I was in this office was last night when I saw out the office cleaners at eight pm.'

'Then how on earth did this letter get here, I wonder?' asked the Governor, perplexed, 'nothing unusual happened last night, I take it?'

'Why of course not, sir,' replied Thomas, getting very agitated, 'all the outer doors to the bank were locked and double locked as usual when I left the building at eight-thirty, then I personally saw the troop of thirty-four Guardsmen in their red jacketed uniforms marching round the building with their rifles on their shoulders guarding the bank, as they have done every night since 1780. Who is the letter from? Is it signed sir?'

'Here, read it for yourself,' Governor Pattison swivelled the open letter round towards the other side of the desk, Thomas put down his box of post and, putting on a wire-held pair of spectacles at the end of his nose, read:

10th June, 1836
Deer Sir,

I have read in my newspaper that the bank of England is the safest place in England. Also my mates in my local pub, The Albion, which is quite close to the bank, always say that anything of value can be left in the vaults of the Bank of England and it will be safe as can be. "As safe as the Bank of England" they say. As a great believer in this country and my allegiance to our King William the fourth, I beg to differ. If you would go to the lowest vaults, the very deepest, on Monday next, at eight pm, I will prove to you that this is not so.

Edward Mulgrave.

'Well, I've never seen anything like it,' Thomas was appalled at what he had just read, 'how can this Mulgrave person prove our bank is not the safest in the country, on any night, never mind next Monday.'

'If that is so,' answered the governor with deadly seriousness, 'then how did he get this letter onto my desk?'

'Good grief, sir, if this is true, what are we to do?' Thomas was shaking with fear and worry, 'what if someone is getting into the bank? How can we apprehend him?'

'I tell you what, Mister Newman,' mused the Governor, in a low, secretive voice, 'let's not start a panic, and keep this to ourselves. We have to sort this out. Tell me, those guards that patrol around this bank building every night, do you know the Captain's name? Or do you, perhaps, actually know him?'

'Well, only to nod to, sir,' explained Thomas, 'just sort of in passing, over the years, you know.'

'Would you get him in here to see me, today?' the Governor asked.

Later that day, there was another tap on the Governor's door, and Thomas Newman ushered in a tall, slim soldier. 'Captain Berryman,' stated Thomas, 'Captain of the Guard for the Bank of England.' Captain Berryman wore a tall black bicorne hat – a hat with two corners, one above each shoulder – his piercing blue eyes looked out under straight eyebrows, and he had a sharp nose and a finely trimmed moustache above a firm-set mouth and clean shaven chin. A pure white wig fell round the side and back of his head, and beneath was the brightest red jacket with gold tasselled shoulders and blue edging and gold buttons. His trousers were of the whitest white and were tucked into shiny black boots with gold tassels. From a white belt at his waist hung a golden handled sword.

The Captain marched to the desk, and saluted formally to the Governor. 'Good Day Sir!' he barked and stood stiffly to attention.

'Good Day Captain, please be seated,' invited the

Governor, 'and read this letter.' He slid the opened letter across his desk. The Captain sat and read with growing consternation.

'He can't do that!' Captain Berryman cried, 'no one can get in the Bank of England. Why, I patrol outside here every night. No-one can get in!'

'Then, pray tell me,' answered the Governor, 'how this person placed a letter on my desk before anyone got here this morning.' The Captain looked hopelessly lost.

'This is what I plan,' the Governor leaned forward in his seat, 'first, tell no-one of this letter. If it got out that someone can walk into this building without being seen, there could be a national panic. Who would trust us, if it is not "As safe as the Bank of England"?

'On Monday next, instead of your usual patrol around the perimeter of the bank, march your men down to the lowest vaults. Hide your soldiers around the vault, with rifles at the ready. Station some of the men at the gas lamps, where they can raise or lower the flame of the lamp. When, and if, this man turns up, we've got him.

'Be ready to shoot him. He could be any type of villain or agent from another country, here to rob us or humiliate us. And do you know this pub, The Albion?'

'I do, sir, I do.' The Captain looked thoughtful, 'you want me to raid it? See if it's full of anti-government dissidents?'

'Definitely not. Get a few of your soldiers to casually visit the pub, dressed in street clothes, not army uniforms. Get them to mingle with the clientele, and find out; what's the conversation in the public bar? What's the political views of the patrons? And find out, who is Edward Mulgrave? Is he a commanding figure, a political orator? A villain?'

'And nab him?' Captain Berryman leaned forward and gripped the handle of his sword, eager to use it.

'No, no.' Governor Pattison thumped his palm down on the desk top, 'watch him, follow him, find out who are his associates, and his political views. We'll get him when and if he gets in my bank. And we must have utter secrecy, no one must find out about this letter or this person. He obviously *can* get in, because of the very presence of this letter. The whole country would be put in a terrible panic if the Bank of England was found to be not completely trustworthy.

'So spy on him, follow him. Then we'll nab him and his gang if he is not alone. Now, please act normally, do your usual patrol round the bank every day until next Monday, when we shall proceed to our lowest vaults with your soldiers at the ready.'

The day-to-day workings of the most famous bank in Britain continued every day until the following Monday, with no information coming from the infiltration from the out-of-uniform soldiers who had frequented *The Albion* pub, and no knowledge of the mysterious Albert Mulgrave.

That Monday evening at seven thirty, Captain Berryman and his armed-to-the-teeth soldiers in their red jacketed uniforms squeezed themselves into the lowest vault of the bank. The soldiers spent many minutes gasping in awe at the glittering rack after rack of beautiful gold ingots which filled all the available floor space, from the ground up to shoulder height, filling the large vault with a golden glow.

With gas lamps all around the walls turned up to full flow, giving the lamps their brightest illumination, the vault was lit up and the flames reflected onto the gold, where the soldiers, in their red jackets and white trousers, each stood carrying a glowing oil lamp in one hand which added to the brilliant light, and a long rifle with fixed bayonet in the other.

Captain Berryman, Governor Pattison and chief clerk Thomas Newman stood to one side. 'Now, gentlemen,' the Governor said in a loud whisper, 'please lower yourselves down, below the height of the gold bars, turn down the gas lamps on the wall to their lowest setting and turn down your oil lamps. When I get any alarm at all that the man has arrived I will shout: NOW! And we can turn our flames up to the maximum and see the fellow in the flesh for the first time. Unless he attacks us, please do not shoot him. I would love to learn what his motives are. And so gentlemen, prepare yourselves!'

The soldiers surrounding the vault and the officer in charge and the bank officials lowered the power of the lamps to a gentle glow and sunk down behind the glowing bars and waited...

Silence descended on the group, accompanied by the occasional cough or sniff from a soldier or a boot sliding on the stone flagged floor. The time ticked slowly by... Nothing hardly moved, the low hiss of the fluttering gas lamps became soothing. Men relaxed in a comfortable position by the bars of gold... Suddenly, a loud clunk! followed by even louder clunks and clicks as the nervous soldiers dragged themselves up and drew back the hammers on their Baker flintlock rifles.

'Wait! Wait!' Governor Pattison held up his hands, then put a finger in front of his lips as he pointed to the culprit of the clunk. All in the vault followed his pointing digit... to a large brown rat scuttling in the corner.

The men settled down once again, clicking closed the hammers on their rifles and sliding down behind the rows of gold bars. Then:

'Good grief!' chief clerk Thomas Newman cried, 'look at the wall!' With a great loud clattering, everyone stood up and stared. A shadowy figure had appeared at the far end of the vault against the wall. Lamps were shone, gas lamps heightened, hammers on rifles were readied and pointed at the man who had suddenly materialised.

The man was small with a little round black leathery hat on his head, where his hair, though cut short fell out from beneath either side. Of middle age and fairly tubby, the man had straight, serious eyes, short nose and an unsmiling mouth on his clean shaven face. He wore a collarless shirt, a black waistcoat with all its buttons open, thick, coarse trousers, held with a strong leather belt, and just below each knee a tight string stopped anything from rising from the waters into his clothing. On his feet were large thick boots. All of his clothing seemed to be filthy with dirt and mud.

'No! Stop!' Captain Berryman held up his hands as he

cried to his troops who seemed about to fire their rifles at the intruder, 'wait until he tells his story.'

'Milords,' spoke the man as he took off his leathery cap, 'Edward Mulgrave at your service.'

'You are the man who sent us the letter,' enquired Thomas Newman, 'the man who can break into and out of the Bank of England at will?'

'Yes, sir.'

'Then you are caught, red handed,' Captain Berryman said drawing his sword, 'then you will see the inside of the Tower of London this very day for your crimes, sir!'

'What crime would that be sir?' Edward Mulgrave stood carefully still, eyeing the soldiers with their aimed rifles, 'I am a sewer worker, and I work here, under the bank of England, and I have worked here for many a year. And some time ago I found a way into the lower vaults through a crack in the wall by the River Walbrook, which is your sewer, it's an ancient London river that runs below this bank and is used as your sewer. It is quite normal for old rivers to be used as sewers, 'cos the rivers always run to the Thames. The river Fleet is another river used as a sewer.

'No sir, I found the crack in the wall some time ago. I could have taken a bar of your gold every day for months now and then I could've disappeared, and you'd never have found me. But I am an honest man, and I believe in my country and my King, and I thought I would show you the place where I got In and you could have it bricked up and then everything in the bank would be "As safe as the Bank of England".

'You know, he's right,' Governor Pattison said with a smile, 'he could have robbed us of a fortune in gold. Instead he informs us of the break in the wall. Mister Mulgrave, please show Captain Berryman where the breach of our defences is, so that it can be repaired, and then Mister Newman will bring you to my office.'

Later in the evening, sewer worker and Bank of England Governor faced each other across the large desk, with Captain Berryman and Thomas Newman standing by. 'Mister Mulgrave,' stated the Governor, 'in respect of your outstanding honesty, the bank has awarded you this:' He counted out into a leather bag the sum of eight hundred pounds. Mister Mulgrave went home a very rich man.

'That was a lot of money,' said Thomas Newman.

'A great deal of money,' added Captain Berryman.

'Yes, I agree,' smiled the Governor, 'he was rewarded for all the good things this bank stands for, which is: *Honesty is the best policy.*'

Legend or Myth

The above fictitious story, and the £800 reward, is loosely based on a legend / myth which is neither denied nor attested by the Bank of England.

CONFUSION

The Burgess brothers sat in the half empty bar of *The Windmill* pub, just off the town's high street, sipping pints of bitter. The pub was situated close to the two room flat that they rented, and although the bar was filled with worn furniture and threadbare carpets, it served beer, so here they sat. The Burgess boys were in their twenties: Alexander "Alex" Burgess, the older of the two was tall with his light brown hair clipped at the sides with a large mop at the top; he had dark eyes, a sharp nose with a fluffy thin moustache and beard. He wore a white long sleeved shirt, tight grey trousers and black soft leather shoes. His younger brother, Bobby, was shorter, thick set with a tangle of dark hair and beneath his short nose was a thick moustache and straggly beard. He wore an old faded blue T-shirt, baggy shorts with a white flower-like pattern and old, dirty white trainers.

'We're skint,' Alex said in a whisper.

'Potless,' answered Bobby, sipping at the half empty glass on the scarred table top.

'It's time to gather in some cash,' Alex mused, 'get some dough together, and this time, get a nice wedge of notes in our pockets.'

'Yeah, we gotta rob a bank, or raid a cash transit van,' Bobby looked excited.

'Or nick another car,' sighed Alex with resign, 'just like we always do.'

'Yeah, OK,' sighed his brother, 'only thing about that, though, is that we keep getting caught, usually sitting in the car we've just nicked.'

'Well, this time,' said Alex, pointing his finger at Bobby, 'I've got a brand new plan.'

'Yeah, OK,' Bobby looked up with a sigh, 'what we gonna do? Nick a motor and then jump out of it before the Old Bill get there? But then we wouldn't have the nicked car, would we?'

'No. No, I worked this out,' Alex began drawing a map in the spilt beer on the table top with his finger, 'you know that row of garages in the alley off Bond Gardens?'

'Course I do, you've rented one of the garages there, number six.'

'Number seven, actually,' corrected Alex.

'Oh, I thought it was number six,' Bobby looked at the map in beer on the table top, 'aint you got an old Ford in that garage? An old eight horsepower Ford, right?'

'Wrong,' sighed Alex, 'it's a ten horsepower Ford, actually. But never mind that; did you know Stan Wellings? Well, it don't matter if you knew Stan or not, but he had a Triumph Stag in garage number six, but he sold his car, and the garage number six was for rent. And I rented it.'

'What's in the garage, Alex?' Bobby was confused, 'how we gonna pay the rental on it?'

'Garage six is now empty, but that's the idea,' smiled Alex, 'next time we nick a motor, we rush it round to the garages, stash it in number six and lock it in. Then, if the coppers come round to see us, we show them garage number seven.'

'Not six?' Bobby ventured.

'No, seven, that's where the old Ford is, in seven, it's well known that that's my garage, number seven. We'll secretly keep number six for us when no one else is around. Then we can go back later and sell the stolen car, pocket the cash and pay the rent on the garage.'

'Great idea,' smiled Bobby, 'and our garage is number six and not number seven.'

'No,' sighed Alex, 'ours is seven, not six. Let's go down there now.' The two slurped down the remainder of beer in their pint glasses and left the pub. They wandered down the house and shop-lined road with its passing red buses, vans and cars, into Bond Gardens, then down the alley into the dead end area where the two rows of identical garages were lined up on either side. All were painted white, with swing-up doors. Above each door was a whitewashed out number, and every garage door had a large padlock at its foot.

'Here we are,' smiled Bobby, giving a secret wink, 'number six.'

'Next door, idiot,' Alex shook his head, 'number seven. Look at the padlock. It hasn't got a key, its got a combination lock, you put in the correct number and the lock pops open.' Alex fiddled with the numbers on the padlock, spinning them around. 'Six, seven, six, seven. There,' he announced. The lock sprang open. They raised the door and saw the old black Ford car inside, with an old bed headboard, plastic bags full of dusty old tools and paint-splashed decorating materials by its side.

'That's a very clever locking thingy,' Bobby said admiringly, looking at the padlock.

'Now check this out,' Alex said with a quick look either way, to see that the rows of garages were deserted, and then moved next door to garage number six, where he raised the padlock on that door and spun the numbers and that lock too, sprung open. He raised the swing up door to show that the interior of the garage was empty.

'Now, here's what I've done,' Alex curled his index finger at Bobby to get him to come over and pay attention, 'look at both these padlocks, both are combination locks, and to make sure that there's no confusion, I have given them both the same combination number, and it is...' he stared hard at Bobby as he spoke, 'six, seven, six, seven, and that's the number for both padlocks. Six, seven, six, seven... Get it?'

'Course, I got it,' Bobby grinned widely, 'Six, seven, six, seven. Hey, that's the number of both our garages as well, aint it? Six and seven, six and seven, and our padlock numbers are the same; six and seven.'

'You got it, you got it.' Alex gave Bobby both padlocks, 'OK, now lock them both up and we'll go looking for a nice new motor to fit into our new empty garage.'

'Erm...' Bobby looked confused as he held both padlocks, 'which one goes where? I mean, which padlock is for garage number six and which is for number seven?'

'That's what I've been telling you,' Alex gasped at his

thick brother, 'they're both the same, they fit both garages, they've both got the combination lock number six, seven, six, seven. So just put the padlocks on, twirl the numbers and let's go!' Bobby put the padlocks in place on the garage doors, twirled the numbers and locked up both garage doors, then the boys were off.

Shortly, the Burgess boys arrived at the local petrol station where they loitered nearby at the automated car wash and peered round the corner at the petrol pumps, hoping for a forgetful person in a hurry, who might leave the ignition keys in the car while they paid for their petrol in the kiosk. But no, after half an hour, Alex and Bobby gave up. 'Let's move on,' said Alex, 'to the shoppers' car park.' They strolled the five hundred metres into Safebuy's supermarket car park.

'Now, we're looking for a nice, clean car,' instructed Alex, 'fairly modern with good tyres. That way we can hide the car in our new garage till things quieten down and the cops are not on the prowl, then take it down to Big Paul's breakers yard where he can dismantle it and sell the parts. After paying us a nice few quid for it, of course.'

After dodging around shoppers who were loading their cars with goods or new shoppers arriving to do their shopping; when no one was looking, the boys tried doors and boot handles, as they toured the lines of parked cars. 'This one's unlocked!' bobby hissed at his brother as he opened the door of an old Vauxhall Astra, 'shall we?'

'Nah, too old and too battered,' sniffed Alex, moving slowly on, as Bobby ducked his head inside the car.

'Hey! Look at this!' Bobby laughed, holding forth an iPad and an old leather purse.

'Stick them in your rucksack, and let's move on.' Alex ordered. From the large pockets of his baggy shorts, Bobby pulled a rolled up rucksack. He unrolled it, put his newly stolen goods inside and after pulling the strings tight, slung it on his back. Then they moved on, along the lines of cars.

Lisa Stanwick hardly slowed down as she raced her Audi S3 into the Safebuy's supermarket car park. She knew she was driving too fast, but she was late: she had had the morning off work to see her mum, and mum had kept her talking too long, and then mum wanted Lisa to pick up her prescription from Safebuy's pharmacy. And Lisa *had* to get the prescription now, because the chemist would be closed when Lisa finished work later. And she was late! Her blonde hair had gone flyaway and her make up and lipstick had faded, and her boss would not be forgiving when she arrived late at work for the afternoon. She skidded the car to a halt and jumped out and walked, as fast as possible in her grey office skirt and jacket with her high heeled shoes, to the supermarket entrance.

As she disappeared through the automatic doors of the store, the two heads of the Burgess boys raised from the other side of her car. Alex slid to one side and tried the door handle, and click! the door opened. Finding the key in the ignition, Alex started up the engine and signalled for his brother to get in the passenger side of the car. As soon as Bobby was half way in the passenger seat, Alex roared the car off with squealing tyres leaving rubber marks on the car park tarmac.

Roaring down the main road, blasting past the buses, vans and cyclists, weaving their way dangerously through the traffic, they made their way to Bond Gardens and skidded down into the row of garages.

Out on the nearby main road, PC Nick Ferrar sat at the wheel of the silver police BMW patrol car with "blues and two" lighting above on the roof and the blue "POLICE" decal on the bonnet. Nick was a keen young officer who sat in his blue uniform shirt and trousers with his jacket and cap behind him in the car. He had cropped black hair, determined steely blue eyes, a slightly flattened nose above a clipped moustache, and a clean shaven chin with bluish stubble.

Next to Nick Ferrar sat WPC Josie Taylor, a tall young girl, fairly new to the Metropolitan Police, with brown hair in a short, tight pony tail, lightly tanned face without make up, brown eyes, with a straight nose and a slight smile showing even, white teeth. She also wore her blue uniform shirt with sleeves rolled up, and uniform trousers. Both officers wore their utility belts with pepper spray and handcuffs.

'Metro one.' The police radio crackled into life, and both Nick and Josie paid immediate attention. 'Metro one,' the radio message began again from the local police station, 'vehicle stolen from Safebuy's car park. An Audi S3, registration number LG68LAC. Stolen not six minutes ago, so should be in your vicinity.'

'OK, Metro.' Josie said into the dash mounted microphone, 'on our way.' The police BMW slid away from the kerb and headed fast into town. 'Maybe the car thieves want to go south and have headed straight for the motorway,' Josie wondered out loud.

'Well if they have,' answered Nick as he steered quickly past a truck on their way into the middle of the town, 'it'll be left for the motorway patrol cars to find them. Let's just go round the high street once or twice to eliminate the local boys.' They circled round the town.

The town seemed fairly quiet. 'Shall we give the garages in Bond Gardens a quick look?' Josie suggested, as they drove near to the road where the garages were located.

'Sure.' Nick expertly spun the steering wheel and they rocketed down to Bond Gardens.

'Quick! Get the garage unlocked!' Alex screamed as the boys thundered to a halt by the garages. Bobby scrambled out and ran to the up and over doors. He grabbed at the padlock and twirled the key numbers 'Six, seven, six, seven.' Bobby gasped out loud as he turned the numbers.

'Not seven!' Alex shouted through the open door of the stolen Audi car, 'Six!'

'Yes, that's what I'm doing!' Bobby wailed, 'you said: Six, Seven, Six, Seven.'

'Yes, that's the padlock number!' Alex screamed, 'but you want garage six and you're opening number seven!' Bobby's eyes nearly popped out of his head when he looked up. He was at the wrong garage! He wanted to open number six and he had automatically opened their own one at number seven. He crashed the padlock back on, twirled the numbers and dived to the garage next door. Then he fumbled with the padlock as Alex turned the stolen car round and aimed it at the garage interior.

Bobby threw open the number seven garage door and Alex roared the car into the empty interior. As soon as the Audi was stopped in the garage, Alex jumped out of the car, ran out of the garage, slammed the slide-down shutter, slipped on the padlock and stood up, just as the police car slid to a stop in the middle of the dead end row of garages.

Nick and Josie climbed slowly out of the patrol car, while the Burgess boys looked on guiltily, standing in front of garages six and seven. 'Well, well, if it isn't the Burgess boys. You rent a garage down here, don't you, boys?' Nick Ferrar asked, turning his back on the boys and facing Josie who was standing by the police car.

'Yes,' the boys said at the same time.

'Which garage is yours?' Nick asked with a serious-faced wink to Josie.

'Sss...' began Bobby.

'Seven,' finished Alex.

'Open up,' demanded Josie, 'right now.'

Alex backed away to the garage, and began to twirl the numbers, 'six, seven, six, seven.' He could hear a strange echo of his reading out of the numbers. Oh no! Bobby was opening up the garage next door! And reading out the numbers as well. 'What are you doing , Bobby?' he cried.

'Opening up number seven... no, six... oh!' Too late. The fold up door opened up to reveal the stolen Audi. 'Oh, sorry Alex,' Bobby said with a sigh, as he heard the handcuffs being drawn out of the copper's belts for him and his brother, 'I've been at sixes and sevens all day.'

6's & 7's

The Livery companies list in the City of London, the list of the most famous and important guilds, and companies in the city, is headed at number one position by The Worshipful Company of Mercers. It was said that at joint sixth in the order of preference stood the Merchant Taylors and the Skinners livery companies. The two trade associations, founded in the same year, argued over this sixth place. In 1484, after much bickering, the Lord Mayor of London decided that the companies would swap between sixth and seventh place in each year. To forget whether your livery is in sixth or seventh position this year is to be confused: you're at sixes and sevens.

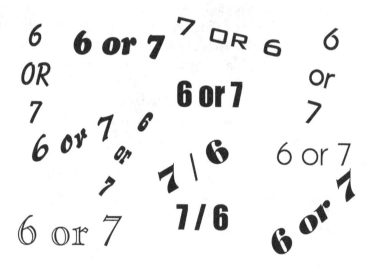

JULIA'S STORY

Julia Thornton walked along the pavement towards the *Coach & Horses* pub on the outskirts of town; she was in her middle twenties, and looked very, very good. Hey, everybody knew she looked good, *she* knew she looked good. Julia was the best looking, most popular girl around. She had long golden hair which flowed to her shoulders, a deep dark tan on her oval face, and had black eyebrows and long lashes around her grey-green eyes. Her pink lips always showed a tiny, secret smile and pearly white teeth. She was tall, slim, and had a great figure. She walked with elegance, confidence and a lot of style.

Julia wore a flowery, loose-fitting half-open top which fell to just below her waist and beneath that were the tightest fitting black leggings that she could just get into. Finishing off her look for this evening was her shiny pink leather hand bag and shiny pink leather shoes with the five inch heels.

She pushed open the door of the pub and strutted in, looking neither to her left nor right. She had no need to see what was going on around her; she knew. At this time in the early evening, the pub was full of young men who had dropped in for a pint or two after work, and as she entered she could just feel the moment of silence as all the men turned to look and gawp at her. She knew they would all stop and look at her, they *always* did. She looked *that* good.

Julia pushed through the bar and out to the garden area of the busy pub where all her gang of friends met on these summer evenings. She hurried through onto the flagstone paved floor to find that only one of her friends – well, a mere follower, really - was already there, Milly, the tubby one with the freckled face and the style less T-shirt and jeans with sandals. 'Hi, Julia,' said Milly breathlessly, in open admiration, 'you look really great.'

'Yeah,' Julia sat in the slatted, white painted chair at one of the white garden tables, and looked in contempt at the neatly kept flowers and plants in the pub garden, with its old-fashioned silver street lamps and flame heaters for when it got chilly.

The bar door opened and Annie, the dark haired young waitress girl from the pub's restaurant, wearing a *Coach & Horses* apron over her black shirt and trousers came into the garden. 'Hi Julia, you look really great,' she said with a smile, 'there's a young man in the bar who wants to buy you a drink. What will you have this time?'

'Cola with ice,' Julia said without turning to look at Annie, as she coolly slipped on her expensive-looking sunglasses.

'There's always a young man who wants to buy you a drink, isn't there?' Milly said with a grin.

'Yeah,' Julia stared into the distance with a smug look, 'there's always a guy who wants to buy me a drink.'

Within a few minutes more friends arrived at the pub garden and sat around Julia; there was Tina and Shirley, both coming in after their working day, dressed in smart office suits with short skirts and "sensible" shoes with low heels. Tony the tall muscle-bound plumber bloke arrived still wearing his overalls with the braces on the shoulders, and unshaven Derek turned up with his crumpled grey suit and scuffed shoes. All sat around Julia's table trying to look cool and listened to what she had to say, the boys hardly taking their eyes off Julia.

Then the crowd around Julia was joined by Carla, the big girl with the brown staring eyes, short-cropped white hair, black eyebrows and big teeth with her white make-up, wearing her long summer flowery patterned dress and flat shoes. 'Hi Julia, you look really great,' she said as she sat at Julia's table by dragging up a chair, 'I saw your boyfriend in the town today.'

'What?' Julia was annoyed, sitting up suddenly, 'what boyfriend?'

'Why, Conner, Conner Collins of course,' answered Carla, surprised.

'Oh, him,' Julia snorted, 'well he's not my boyfriend any more. He's had his chance. I'm chucking him today.' The surrounding young people gave a sudden gasp, what an exciting and dramatic life Julia had, changing things, and boyfriends at a whim.

'Conner Collins,' Julia snorted in disgust, 'I'd call him Conner Careful. I've been going out with him for three months. He's got a tiny little car, because it's cheap to run, but he's saving up and in time he's going to have a big car. He does the lottery each week – just in case his numbers come up – even though it's a fifteen million to one gamble. He collects pictures... pictures would you believe! of Rolls-Royces! pictures! He hasn't got one, a Rolls-Royce, no, but he has got a lot of pictures of them.

'When he took me out for a meal, it had to be before six o'clock in the evening so we could get an early bird meal for half price, he says he'll take me to a good posh restaurant when he can afford it.

'Last week he asked me if I'd go away on a week's holiday with him...'

'Well, you like a nice holiday,' commented one of the boys, 'a week in Spain or Portugal.'

'Huh! Spain or Portugal!' she spat, 'he wanted me to go to Bognor! staying in a caravan! With his mum! He said we'd have to save up and go abroad in a few years time, until then we could go to his mum's caravan. He can get lost.'

'When I saw Conner today,' continued Carla, 'he said he had something to tell you.'

'Well, if he wants to tell me,' giggled Julia, 'that he loves me and wants to marry me, I'll laugh in his face! I'm the one girl that can have any bloke I like, the one that they all look at when I pass. I can get a guy to take me to the best restaurants in a flash car or a taxi. And take me on holiday in the best resorts, in the sun. I'll tell Conner Careful to...'

'Oh! Here he is,' one of the girls cried as Conner walked through the door of the pub. A sudden silence fell over the whole of the group as Conner rounded onto Julia's now crowded table. Conner was of medium height, with dark hair cut quite short, dark eyebrows, bright brown eyes and with a shortish nose, straight set mouth and slight dark stubble on his firm chin. He wore an open neck white shirt under a v neck blue pullover, tight grey trousers and black shoes.

'Hey, Julia,I want to tell you...' he said with a smile as he approached Julia's table.

'Hey yourself,' Julia retorted, 'if you think I've been waiting here for you, you've got another think coming. Three months I've been going out with you and all I've got to show for it is an offer of a week in Bognor, and a ride in a little toy car.'

'Well, I was saving...' Conner explained.

'Well, don't save yourself up for me, mister,' she laughed, 'you've had your chance.'

'Oh...OK,' Conner looked around him at the silent gawping faces of the group around the table. 'if you're chucking me, well, I understand that, of course.'

'Well I am chucking you. Anyway, what was it you wanted to tell me today?' Julia said loudly for all to hear.

'Oh, yes,' Conner said just as loudly, 'I wanted to tell you that I've won twelve million pounds on the lottery. I would have come round earlier to tell you, but I was at the Rolls-Royce showroom choosing my car.'

Conner gave a wave to the open-jawed Julia and went out to his Rolls.

Delusions of grandeur

A false and exaggerated belief about one's status or importance.

BOMBER

The battered white Ford Transit van raced noisily into the car park of the Morestar Shopping Mall, splashing through the puddles from the earlier rain that had poured in the morning. Swerving round the cars parked in the tarmac-covered parking lot, the old van scraped many vehicles as it bustled passed. Some people who were just arriving at the mall or loading up their shopping and getting ready to go home were surprised and angered by the roaring and scraping van. 'Oi!' cried one angry old boy, observing the damage to his car, cloth cap covering his balding head, with full, white moustache and beard, blue roll neck jumper and grey slacks with suede shoes.

'Oi!' The man repeated as he began to run, following the white van across the tarmac, which had now come to a skidding stop near the entrance to the mall. Its occupants got out of the van just as the old man approached. He also came to a stop, standing and looking in horror at what he saw, his mouth open, his eyes wide.

Three men had alighted from the Transit, and all wore dark coloured woolly balaclava helmets covering their heads, just revealing sockets for dimly seen eyes and mouth, and dark blue overalls which were buttoned at the neck and reached and fastened down to each wrist and to the ankle, where they wore combat boots. Hanging by a leather belt around each man's waist was a scabbard holding a bayonet, and each man carried a Kalashnikov AK47 assault rifle at the ready in his hands, and each rifle had a forty shell magazine.

The last gunman to alight from the van slowly turned to stare at the cloth capped man, then looked at his AK47 to check that it was locked for single shot and not automatic firing. He then fired twice at the stopped man. Bang! Bang! The rifle spat. The cloth cap man fell dead on the tarmac.

A few of the people in the car park saw, heard, or noticed that *something* was going on, but on hearing the sharp noise of the shots, dived for their cars and drove off in a panic, as others stood frozen with fear, while some fell to the ground and hoped not to be seen by whomsoever was lurking with a gun.

The three men approached the shopping mall. As they neared the entrance, they blasted the automatic glass doors with half a dozen bullets; the medium calibre shells roared from the rifles and spun through the air smashing the glass doors with great crashing sounds before them.

Inside the mall, the noise said all anyone needed to know: gunshots! There was massive panic, as shoppers and staff alike tried to get themselves and their children as far as possible from the three rifle waving men who had just burst into the mall, spraying bullets.

The gunmen walked abreast through the start of the mall until they came to a coffee shop on the right where the nearest gunman walked in and sprayed bullets crashing into the afternoon tea drinkers, killing people at their tables, who had been unable to escape quickly enough. Glass tables smashed to the floor as bullets crashed into people and smashed stainless coffee machines wide open.

The gunman on the left of the three turned his gun and fired indiscriminately into a hairdressers salon, spraying death at the people sitting under hair-dryers or still undergoing treatment. Mirrors and styling devices were smashed and exploded in the noise and confusion.

Vince Burners, the plump security guard who had been at the mall's main entrance just before it had burst into a million pieces of exploding glass, now turned and sprinted, arms outspread, peaked cap on the back of his head, grey uniform of white shirt, grey waistcoat and trousers stained with sweat. 'Run! Run!' Vince shouted at the crowds of shoppers, amid the sound of booming bullets, while he ripped a radio from his belt and screamed at his security office in the lower levels of the mall to call the police and report an ongoing gun attack in the building... Vince suddenly fell to his knees, looking down in surprise at the blood stains which had appeared on his chest, from the shells which had hit him from the gunmen following behind. Vince then fell onto his face.

Alarm bells began to shrill non-stop as fire doors and escape exits were slammed open, followed by crowds of screaming, panicking people, children, prams and wheelchairs. On the sound system, a pre-recorded voice spoke in a warm, friendly male voice: 'The Mall is now closed. Please leave by the nearest exit or entrance...'

As the people screamed and ran, pulling with them children and older members of the public, booming shots were fired into the running people, killing them as they ran, as people dashed away, trampling on those that had fallen; ran out of doors and still kept running as far as they could, they called on their mobiles; the police were on their way. An armed response unit was racing there, and a helicopter was flying towards them.

The gunman knew the police would soon be there and continued to fire at the shoppers, and the plate glass windows of the shops and the fluorescent lighting to kill and create panic.

Their plan was to escape through the delivery entrances at the back of the mall into the loading bay, then scale the dividing wall into the block of flats next door - the Bradmore Estate - then through to the back of the flats, where an empty van awaited them. Then, once into the van, they were gong to drive round to the front of the shopping mall again and attack the police from behind.

On the first floor of the adjoining block of council-owned apartments in the Bradmore Estate, old Frank "Bomber" Hamden stepped out of his small apartment, turned, locked the door, then tried to open it by pulling at the letter box. Satisfied that the door was locked securely, he turned again and faced the handrail of the balcony and looked down at the half empty car park below. He sniffed the air and began to walk down the balcony towards the stairs. A lot of noise was coming from the shopping mall next door to the flats, as though there had been a mad rush in some sort of special sale or maybe a live show was going on, with lots of shouting and jeering.

Frank, or Bomber, as he was known, was eighty three years old, straight backed and upright. His thinning hair was grey and trimmed short, his grey-green eyes were clear and keen, his nose was sharp, his smile always ready, showing old but clean teeth. His skin was dark, as though he had just returned from a foreign holiday, but in fact was a result of many years in hot weathered countries in a long military life.

Bomber wore a dark red short sleeved shirt, black trousers and soft, comfortable black and white trainers. He tapped his way along the balcony with a thin but heavy black stick with a weighty metal end. He was healthy and fit, but needed the slight help of the stick after a bad wound in his leg during his long, long military career.

Many folk in the town knew popular Bomber, and plenty thought that his nick-name "Bomber" came from his still favourite past-time; lawn bowling. When bowling, Bomber tended to bounce his bowls along the grass, causing some to think that he was bombing the green. This was wrong; Frank Hamden had actually been a bomber, the pilot of a Royal Air Force bomber airplane.

During his service with the Royal Air Force he had been prominent in the sports field and became a champion sword fencer and boxer. He had served in many arenas of war around the world, always proud to fight for his country, and had flown many missions deep into enemy territory.

On one such mission, when he was much younger, he had been flying over the Asian jungle landscape of Timobar, a small country whose despotic leader, Kank Dek, had grabbed power from a weak government. Kank Dek announced that he was not going to stand for his country of Timobar to be used by all the western allied governments as a military base. For the future of his country, he said, he had commandeered all foreign military bases, manned them with his own soldiers and would attack any interfering countries with his commandeered nuclear weapons.

After many killings of western troops, war had been declared on Kank Dek. And now a half-hearted truce was in place with small attacks taking place as the world wondered what would Kank Dek do next? Would he use nuclear weapons? On his mission over Timobar Frank began looking for an enemy military airfield he had been sent to neutralise, when his plane was suddenly hit by a ground anti-aircraft attack and had burst into flames.

He parachuted out of his aircraft and landed deep in enemy territory in the dense jungle. Unfastening and freeing himself from the parachute harness, Frank assessed his situation: alone and armed only with the automatic pistol at his hip, with no radio to call for help and he was now kilometres deep into enemy territory, he also had a rudimentary survival kit of some food rations and a small compass stowed in his flying suit. He checked his compass: it was broken.

Bomber had approached this small country from the south, so all he could do was aim himself at the south and walk. He looked up from the lush, green ground that he stood on amid the trees, shrubs and bushes, observed the sun's trajectory and turned south. He marched at a steady rate, not knowing what lay ahead.

He trudged on and on, in the jungle, just aiming vaguely towards the south. Sniffing the strange odours from the weird plants that he was ploughing through, his uniform overalls protecting him from poisons or resins that the scratches from those plants might bring. He wished that he hadn't thrown away his pilot's helmet along with his parachute, which would have saved him from the intense heat of the oppressive sun which beat down with a vengeance, but it had been too uncomfortable and hot to wear.

As night fell, Frank stopped when it was too dark to carry on, and huddled down at the base of a green tree, drew his hands and arms around himself and closed his eyes in exhaustion, as the cold night air crept in.

In the complete darkness of the undergrowth, he felt

something brush by, a soft fur oozing by his arm. He immediately blinked awake, but could see nothing. Then the noises of the night jungle began: the howling of a faraway animal, and then again; was it closer this time? Then the swish of nearby bushes as something whizzed by. Did the grass flatten with a gentle rustle as something slithered passed?

In the morning he uncomfortably raised himself and marched on towards the south. He had to be extremely careful; any natives he encountered would be hostile, he knew. This whole country was against the West.

He had to get back to the British base on the island of Tolsleng where he had flown from, without being seen. He didn't know what he would do when he got to the coast, steal a boat perhaps? He'd try. He marched all day, hungry and his throat burnt with thirst. Late in the afternoon, he came across his first village, where he hid in a clump of bushes and hoped to see some water for the taking, and maybe a crust of bread?

The village was merely bamboo huts with great green leaves woven together for roofs, the sallow skinned people looked thin and as hungry as him, as they seemed to chew on roots and plants. He moved quietly on.

Again, when night approached, he lay shivering on the hot hard ground and fell into a fitful sleep.

As the next early morning sun began to burn his head, Frank stood shakily and trudged on. He moved some large green leaves out of his way, and cool, clear water poured from the leaves onto his face! It was like an ice pack on his face and head. Of course! It was water from the morning dew. Frank gathered many of the leaves and twisting them into a cup shape, drank gratefully. Then he poured more of the dew water over his head, then wove the large leaves into a sun hat for himself.

He walked on into the fierce heat, and after an hour or so, he needed water once again. His trousers were now torn at the ankles, his facial skin mite-bitten and raw, his rations had all been eaten and he just could not find more water. He stumbled wearily on, forcing to place one foot in front of the other, his ankles and calves red raw and scratched by the strange thistle that brushed his torn clothing as he walked. As his strength left him in the blistering heat of the day and the freezing cold of the night, he couldn't remember how many days he had trudged. That night, as he lay on the ground, he wondered if he would ever see his wife and family again, or ever return to England. He eventually fell into a restless fever of a sleep.

When he next awoke, Frank felt relaxed and comfortable, just like waking up in a comfortable bed in the morning and realizing that it isn't a work day. His head was propped up and just as he opened his eyes a large wooden bowl was placed at his lips. He drank a cool, clear almost icy water. He relaxed back for a moment, then looked up. Was this a dream? Was he going to wake up with a parched throat and hunger stretching his aching body?

He opened his eyes once more, and this time found that he had indeed had a cool drink and felt much refreshed. He blinked and saw a man sitting on the grass in front of him. It was a native man with the same deep sallow complexion as the natives of this country, and he had tight braided dark grey hair, small dark eyes on a tubby face with a grey moustache that looked out of place on a native in the jungle. The man had a small blob of a nose above the moustache which made him look like someone's dad or granddad who's just got home from work. He was almost covered in a small blanket with his naked arms and legs showing, and held in his right hand a long thin black stick of about eighty centimetres long with a rounded handle at the top and a metal end at the other. 'Who...' Frank spoke.

The man raised his left hand for silence, then whispered, 'Relax my friend, my name is Pul Ret and I am not your enemy.' The man disappeared into the undergrowth, later to return with more cool water for Frank to drink, some fruit and a small piece of cooked meat. He ground some plants into a bowl and smeared the mixture onto Frank's burnt and raw face, arms and legs. Frank felt better as the mixture affected his skin, making it feel stronger. Then the man made Frank a new hat out of large green leaves.

'Now we can talk,' said the man in a clear, slightly accented voice as he sat back down again, 'you are the Bomber?'

'The Bomber? Oh, yes, the bomber,' answered Frank, 'I was the pilot of the bomber that was shot down. I suppose that you are going to turn me in to your military?' He surreptitiously felt for the pistol at his hip.

'Well, I think that you should come with me,' said Pul Ret. Frank pulled the gun from his belt. With a movement as fast as a blink of the eye, Pul Ret swung the black stick, and with a click, the pistol was knocked out of Frank's hand. 'I said I was not your enemy, Bomber, but if you try to attack me again, you will die.' The black stick returned with a flash to Pul Ret's side.

'I think that you should come with me,' continued Pul Ret as if nothing had happened, 'because I can get you to the coast and possibly get a boat for you to return to the British Base on the island of Tolsleng.

'Like most people in the western world, you do not understand what is happening in Timobar. Our leader Kank Dek is convinced that by using the West's own weapons against the countries who had placed them there, he would gain world prominence as countries learned to fear Timobar, and send monetary aid and military might to us. But he scours the country searching for young men and women, men to be soldiers of the Timobar military and women to be their wives. He allows no one to have an education, as they might question him and his methods if they were wise in the ways of the world.

'That is why you see the many small villages filled with young people, hidden in the jungle where Kank Dek's men can't find them and force them to join the military, as those of my countrymen who won't join Kank Dek are executed. Kank Dek's men will also be looking for a bomber pilot who might be trying to escape the country...'

For the next four days, Pul Ret and the Bomber walked

and walked, Pul Ret's blanket of the night was now wound round his waist and covered him to his knees. When they passed a small village made up of the population who were keeping away from the army of Kank Dek, Pul Ret would enter quietly and return with a few mouthfuls of food and some water, and still they walked.

At long last they neared the coast, where the jungle and vegetation dropped away to be replaced by a sandy beach and wooden jetties, lined with boat houses and small huts by the waterside, and tied to the jetties were small fishing boats, inflatable dinghies with outboard motors and some sailing boats.

They entered the harbour village carefully, Bomber wearing only a similar waist-to-knee covering as Pul Ret and not much else, as his pilot's clothes would have given him away quickly to the army guards who patrolled the coast line on the beach and in the wooden boats with outboard motors, looking for any escapees from their army or their leader.

No one took any notice of two extra men in the bustling harbour as boats were unloaded, nets were mended and battered old vans and trucks arrived or left the harbour side. All the people at the harbour were old men; too old for Kank Dek's army, as the younger men had disappeared from the soldiers patrolling the coastline. Bomber was now dirty, dusty and sunburned enough to mix in with the locals, as long as he didn't have to speak.

Pul Ret and the Bomber strolled along the edge of the harbour, peering into each of the boat houses that they passed. In most of the wooden framed and leaf-roofed places they saw an old boat used for fishing or for sailing round the coast.

'Ahh, here we are,' Pul Ret whispered as they entered another boat house, 'this is what we've been looking for.'

'This is it?' Bomber asked, 'but it's empty, and there's no door. We can see right out onto the open sea.'

'Yes, we'll wait,' Pul Ret gestured to a log just at the waters edge inside the boat house, 'I'll get us some fruit to eat.' He went out into the surrounding huts and soon returned with fruit. They sat on the log, and they waited. As time went by, it slowly got dark.

Still they waited. The tiny village by the harbour was quiet as all the old men had disappeared off. Then they heard it. A faint buzzing sound of an outboard motor. The buzzing got louder as it drew nearer. Pul Ret stood to one side of the boat house, hidden in the shadows. 'Be ready with your gun!' he hissed. 'it is Kank Dek's soldier's and they are looking for you. They will kill you on sight.' Bomber pulled out his pistol and quietly readied it for action, as the tension mounted.

Bomber sat at the back of the wooden structure looking out at the moonlit water beyond the open front of the boathouse. Slowly the front of a Timobar military speedboat edged into sight. It turned into the boathouse, the buzzing motor now loud. In the outboard-powered boat stood three uniformed guards, their dark skinned faces grim, wearing their brown outfits with peaked caps. All three had rifles held by a strap over their shoulders, as one of them steered the boat by a central steering wheel.

'Hai! Hai!' one of the guards cried angrily. They all unslung their guns and aimed at Bomber.

'Fire! Fire!' shouted Pul Ret as the three guardsmen began to shoot their rifles into the boathouse. The wooden building shook with many blasts of pistol and rifle shots. Bomber fired his pistol at the three guards until it was empty of shells. Bomber had hit one guard, the steersman, who fell out of the boat backwards into the water. Pul Ret had at the time of the start of the shooting, jumped out at the guards, the black stick swinging over his head with a fearful wooshing sound, it slashed down fully on one of the guards' head, killing him instantly with its iron tip.

Then Pul Ret swung the stick and poked the next guard in the stomach with a heavy blow. As the man doubled over in pain Pul Ret swept at the man's head with the stick like a baseball player. Whack! He too followed into the water with a great splash. 'Pul! Pul!' Bomber cried, 'we've done it...' But Pul Ret was sitting down on the water's edge in the boathouse, blood running from his chest and stomach.

'Pul Ret!' Bomber ran to his friend's side, 'we can make it, we can...'

'No, no, my friend,' whispered Pul Ret, 'I cannot. But you must go. See if you can get to your people. Tell them about me and my countrymen, about our leader, Kank Dek and his tyrant ways. Save our people from him and his vicious army... Tell the world about him, for what he has done to my people, he must face the music. Take my precious stick, it is now your only weapon. Go! Go now! I can hear the buzzing of more shore patrol boats. You must go now...' Pul Ret handed the black stick, with weakened hands slippery with blood, to Bomber, his eyes glassy, his mouth spilling blood as his life ebbed away. 'Keep the stick, it will protect you... I can hear the buzzing of more shore patrols, they must have heard the shots...' his voice now hardly a whisper.

Bomber looked at his friend, the man who had saved him so he could get help for his suffering people. He made a very difficult decision, stood up, grabbed the black stick, jumped into the boat and pulled it out of the boathouse by hanging onto the sides of the wooden building. It was only then that he winced with pain and felt the warm blood ooze from a bullet hole in the lower part of his left leg. Once out into clear water, he put the outboard motor on full power and fled out into the open sea. As he went, he found an oily rag at the rear of the boat which he tied tightly round his leg to hold back the bleeding.

As he drove through the water, further and further from the shoreline, he could hear the angry buzzing of the outboard motors of the new arrivals of armed shore patrol boats in the darkness. He didn't look back; he didn't know how much fuel he had or how long it would last, he just had to get as far away from the coast as he could.

A few hours later in the middle of a seemingly great ocean, the engine sputtered to a stop, out of fuel. In the ensuing silence, the boat was rocked from one side to the other as it drifted in the heavy seas. Bomber scoured the empty night behind him, but none of the shore patrol boats had followed his boat out into the open sea. Now all he could do was wait and hope that a passing ship or boat would pick him up and that it would be a British Navy ship and not a Timobar vessel, before he bled to death from the wound in his leg.

As the helpless little boat was slapped by the waves and the current, rocking it from side to side, Bomber slid into a semi-sleep, eyes half closed, one hand on the blood-soaked rag on his leg, his head rocking back and forth.

Suddenly his head jerked up. He could hear it! A throbbing. A buzzing! He swivelled in his seat to peer behind him into the early morning haze. Were the patrol boats coming after him? The noise got louder, but still the sea was empty. Then he saw it! A helicopter flying nearby. He stood in the moving boat and waved his arms. All he could hope for was that it was a friendly air force chopper that he could see.

The helicopter circled above him and he could see the British insignia on its side. They lowered a cable down to him with a man at its end, who bundled Bomber into a harness and up they went, Bomber clinging to his black stick.

Back at base Bomber told of his story of Pul Ret and his down trodden people, and of the leader of the country, Kank Dek. After telling and re-telling his story to his superiors, and much medical attention, Bomber was shipped back home to Britain, and three months later he learned, Kank Dek and his top brass were all killed by an allied rocket attack. Timobar was liberated, and stripped of its weapons. Soon after with some help from the West, it began a new life of peaceful agriculture and trade.

Time went on and as the years passed, Bomber, still with Pul Ret's black stick, eventually retired from the armed forces. His family grew up and when his wife of many happy years died, he moved into the flat by the shopping mall, near the home of his daughter Evie, who met him for lunch in the mall each week to see that he was alright. Bomber became known as the friendly old boy with the black walking stick.

Pheep – pheep – pheep! The mobile phone in his pocket began to send painfully high-pitched whistling pheeps into his ears as he approached the thick, swing door that led to the concrete stairs leading from his first floor landing to the ground. 'ullo. Ullo!' Bomber spoke into the small telephone that his daughter insisted that he carry with him at all times.

'Dad! Dad!' came the voice of his daughter Evie, 'don't meet me in the mall...' her voice was drowned out from the other side of the mall by the roaring of the helicopters, police sirens, the shouting and screaming of the crowds escaping from the shopping area, 'three terrorist gunmen... shooting... guns... killing innocent passers-by...' the line went dead.

'What? This can't be happening...' Bomber pocketed the phone, went through the swing door and began to walk down the stairs to the ground floor, 'I can't leave Evie somewhere where she may be in danger.' He would go and investigate.

As Bomber descended the stairs, and was nearly at ground level, he saw his neighbour old Charlie Smithers passing the entrance way, from right to left, Charlie wore as usual his ancient army beret over his dark, lined old face and his usual blue suit, but he was – walking backwards! 'Chas...?' Bomber's words froze in his throat as Charlie, still backing away from something, looked up at Bomber. His eyes were filled with fear. Bomber froze on the third step of the staircase as Charlie backed just a step more, when the end of a rifle appeared, closing in on Charlie's head. Boom! The rifle was fired at point blank range and Charlie dropped dead to the floor without a sound.

More of the rifle appeared, then the hooded head; the man saw on his left a flicker of movement on the stairs. Too late. Bomber's black stick slashed through the air over the man's head and the heavy metal end crashed down on his skull. He dropped next to Charlie, never to get up again by his own movement. The rifle clattered next to him and Bomber kicked it away.

Boom! A shot whistled over Bomber's head. He spun

33

round to see another gunman in the same balaclava top and outfit as the one he had just felled. Through the open mouthpiece of the Balaclava Bomber could see the grin of hatred on the mouth of the man inside, as he raised his rifle again. Bomber staggered back into the staircase and scrambled up the stairs with the aid of his stick. At the top of the stairs, Bomber pushed very hard at the swinging door on his right to his balcony but slipped through the other swing door on the left, leading to the other side of the flats.

The gunman followed instantly, running up the stairs two at a time. He espied the still swinging door on the right and kicked it open, and fired his rifle along the balcony, Boom! Boom! Just then Bomber emerged from the *other* swing door and with all his might, Bomber smashed his stick, sword-like into the man's kidneys. 'Eeeaaggghhh!' the gunman screamed, dropping his weapon which clattered down the concrete stairs. Bomber swung the stick as far as he could over his left shoulder, then brought it round in a great arc and slashed it on to the man's head. With a mighty grunt the man followed his rifle down the stairs and laid still.

'Three!' Bomber said out loud, 'Evie said *three* terrorist gunmen... there's one more,' he clattered back down the stairs and along to the dividing wall from the flats to the back of the shopping mall. As he approached, a hand appeared on the top of the wall, followed by another hand, this time grasping a rifle. And now Bomber could hear the noise of the wailing crowd as they fought to escape the carnage in the mall, while some people angrily braved the gunmen and fought back in anger.

Bomber then saw the man's head pop up at the top of the wall. 'You're the third and last,' Bomber said to the man, 'and for what you've done, you must face the music,' as he thrust his black stick end, hard! deep into the man's left eye. The man dropped to the ground with a scream as blood poured from his empty eye socket. He fell back into a waiting crowd who exacted their revenge and tore him to pieces.

Bomber cleaned his stick on the jacket of the fallen

gunman who lay near old Charlie, and went to find Evie.

No one ever found out who had stopped the gunmen, and Bomber just carried on with his quiet life.

To Face the Music

It is sometimes said that the saying: 'face the music' originated from the tradition of disgraced army officers being "drummed out" of their regiment for some major offence. Another popular theory is that it was from the theatre where actors who "faced the music", that is, faced the orchestra pit, when they went on stage.

'Bomber'

THE BIG WIG!

Ernie Bristow parked his old green motorbike outside the tiny factory of Pearsall's Plastic Packaging Limited in one of the endless brick-built back streets of the Lenfold Industrial Estate. He switched off the smoky engine of the bike and pushed it by its sellotaped-up saddle to lean against the factory wall. He took off his ancient white crash helmet, pushed open the factory's front door, and stepped inside.

Ernie hung his crash helmet on a rusty nail which protruded from the wall, and peeled off his old waterproof coat and gloves that he wore for riding his bike and hung them on a coat hangar which was on a nearby water pipe. Ernie was tall with flattened back, very dark hair and had brown eyes under a wrinkly forehead, with a sharp nose and firm mouth on a stubbly chin. He wore a white long-sleeved shirt, blue trousers and scuffed black shoes.

Now in his fiftieth year, and after many previous jobs, this was Ernie's new attempt to be the manager of a firm, to be the man in charge and to get people to do what he told them to do, which had been the reason for many of his previous let-downs at other firms. This was his first day as manager of this tiny factory.

The empty "factory" that he saw inside the building was in fact just one unit, a square box of brick walls and a corrugated roof, with the front entrance he had just walked through with another door over in the back wall, doubling as fire exit and way out to the loading bay. The walls were covered with yellowed and peeling metallic pages announcing; "Factory Acts", "What to do in an Accident", and "First Aid" with a few old photographs and long forgotten hand written notices.

Outside in the loading bay was a large shed which contained many hundreds of coat hangers and plastic carrier bags, monogrammed with different high street store logos, and it was here in Pearsall's Plastic Packaging, or PPP, as it was known, that the hangers were boxed up and parcelled, and sent on to the high street stores, so that each store handed out hangars and carrier bags with their own logo printed on its side.

There were four worktop benches in the tiny factory where the packaging staff took hangers and bags from the store outside and re-packaged them for delivery to the appropriate department store. Each bench was covered with the packaging, sellotape and labels that the last person working on the bench had left when their shift ended last Friday evening at the end of the working day. Each bench had a wooden seat for the worker to sit on, except one, which had a small box in front of it.

In the far right corner of the workplace was a small cubicle containing a large kettle, tea bags, a tiny fridge for the milk and lots of labels, pens, brooms, mops and buckets, as this was the domain of the long term employee of PPP, Joseph Pearson, an old boy, Ernie had been told.

Ernie stood by one of the benches, rolled up his sleeves and checked his wrist watch: eight forty-five. Now he'd see who was on time and who would be getting their first rollocking for being late! Ernie stood, tapping his fingers on the bench top, a wicked grin on his face as the minutes ticked by...

Click! Eight fifty. The door opened, and in stepped a small wizened old man, who had just a few grey hairs on his head above an old, lined face with dark eyes, bent nose with a narrow chin. He wore an old jumper above a crumpled shirt, with blue coveralls featuring shoulder braces, and old shiny black boots. 'Good morning,' he said with a smile.

'Morning.' Ernie answered curtly, 'I'm the new manager, Mister Bristow, and you are?'

'Joseph Pearson,' smiled the old man, 'I answer the telephone, receive goods in, hand out orders and make the tea, sorry, did you say your name was Ernie?'

'It's *Mister* Bristow.' Ernie dismissed Pearson with a wave as the door opened once more. Eight fifty-two.

A woman had just turned up. She looked middle-aged and was quite tall and thinly built with short brown hair, white, slim pasty face with no make up, brown eyes, and a straight mouth. She wore a white blouse with baggy black trousers and flat black shoes. Her left arm was extremely thin and the fingers were curled up. 'Good morning,' she said, holding her left arm with her right hand, 'I'm Elaine Croft, one of your packers.'

'And I'm your new boss,' Ernie snapped, 'go to your bench, and what's this, how do you pack with a dodgy arm? How many packages did you send out last Friday?'

'Eleven...' Elaine Croft bit her lip and went to the last bench in the small unit as Ernie shook his head at her in distaste.

Click. The door again. Eight fifty-five. A tall young man stepped through. He was big, plump and quite bald for a youngster, and had bulgy grey eyes, button nose and a wet mouth set in a round face. He wore an old green shirt with sleeves rolled up, and loose trousers and tatty old white trainers. He nervously flicked his eyes at Ernie, then quickly looked away.

'I'm your new boss and you must be Greg Tyler. Bench.' Ernie pointed towards the benches and Greg shuffled away, glad to be out from under that fierce scrutiny.

Click. The door. Eight fifty-eight. Just in time! The latest person was a small young black woman with short black hair with larger than life brown eyes, magnified by the lenses of her glasses. She had a short stubby nose with a big lipstick-covered smile showing large even teeth, and wore a blue T-shirt, black leggings and slip on blue shoes. She gently padded her way along to a bench where she stood on a small box so she could easily reach her worktop. 'Hello, new boss,' she smiled, 'I'm Susan Redford, and I'm not late. Sometimes I am a bit late, but you see I look after my son Peter, he's got learning problems and sometimes it's hard to leave him...'

'And I'm your new boss, Mister Bristow,' Ernie said, 'so, all stand by your benches and I'll talk.'

As his motley crew stood behind their usual bench, Ernie thought about his own working life. He had had many different manager's jobs in his time, as he had always wanted to be in charge and tell people what to do and how to do it. He liked to jab out his finger to make a point, demand respect, and tell people where they had gone wrong. This had of course on many occasions brought on bad feelings and on many shop floors he had been asked to leave, because of his domineering behaviour. Well, this time he'd show them! He was going to knock this little work force into shape and get the boss, Mister Pearsall, who he had only talked to over the telephone, to appreciate that he, Ernie Bristow was the bees knees of a manager.

'Right.' Ernie stated as his new staff stood at their benches looking worried, 'as I said, I'm *Mister* Bristow, I'm the new manager of Pearsall's Plastic Packaging Limited, I'm the big cheese, the bigwig. What I say – you do. I'm going to make this little establishment the best in the business, and if you don't make the grade with me – out you go. Now, get to work.'

Ernie turned away and began packaging hangers and carrier bags without looking up again. His new staff stared for a moment then all of a fluster, began to charge into the loading bay to get supplies to start packaging.

Old Joseph Pearson shrugged his shoulders and lit the gas under the large kettle in his little cubicle and brewed some tea. When he had made and poured the tea, Joseph took a tray and loaded it with steaming mugs and toured the little workshop handing them out. When he got to Ernie's bench, he whispered, 'you know, Mister Bristow, there's no need to bully the staff...'

'Listen old man,' snarled Ernie, 'that speech wasn't just for them packagers, it goes for you, too. You don't like it here – out you go.' So the day dragged on, everyone in fear of the brutish new bigwig, all trying to show they could handle more work. By five-twenty, they were all tired out, but Mister Bristow looked at them with a fearful glance if they looked up at the old clock on the wall, before five-thirty on the dot.

And so the days dragged on, when on most days, little Susan Redford would stand as tall as she could from the box that she stood on and say, 'look, Mister Bristow, I have to pick up my son Peter from the day centre...'

'Five-thirty's your time,' Ernie Bristow would warn, then

turn to Elaine Croft and say: 'and Miss Elaine, how many packages have you done today?'

'E-e-eleven,' Elaine would stutter and look down at her withered arm.

'Eleven! Wow, a kid could do better,' Ernie Bristow would say in disgust, 'And you, Mister blubby Greg Tyler, I hope you haven't been dreaming all day.' Greg would look embarrassed and ungainly, then begin to sweat and look close to tears. This happened every day, with the staff of PPP becoming very unhappy most of the time, while old Joseph brought orders and labels to the benches and lugged away filled orders to the loading bay, all the time muttering to himself.

Then one Friday it happened. Susan was tidying up, looking forward to going home, when Ernie Bristow glared at her. 'What's your game madam? D'your glasses need cleaning?' he demanded, 'it's not yet ten to five! Get back on your little box and on with the next order, or out...'

'...Out I go.' Susan flared back, 'well, out I go then. I've had enough. Enough of your bullying. My son Peter may have his problems, but one of them is not a complete disregard for everyone else. All the poor boy wants to do is look at his motor car magazines, he never makes a sound, he just needs me. So that's what he's going to get. I'm off, never to come back. It's been a horrible experience working with you *Mister* Bristow, and I'm glad not to have to see you again.'

'Susan! Susan' old Joseph jumped out from his cubicle, hands raised, 'please think again.'

'No. No, she's right,' the tall, thin Elaine spoke up, 'he is a horrible man, and I could be unemployed and on permanent sickness benefit because of my arm, but I want to earn my place in society by working, but this is too much. I'm leaving with Susan.' Ernie Bristow looked on red-faced as the two women made their way across the factory floor, when Greg Tyler shyly lifted his hand at arms length, to speak.

'At the church hall on Sunday's, they teach that we should all get on together with peace and understanding,' he announced carefully, 'and I can't live like this, near to tears all the time. Goodbye Mister Bristow.' As Greg walked towards the door to join the two ladies, he did something he hadn't done since Ernie started at PPP: he smiled.

'Just a minute,' cried Joseph, 'ladies, Greg. See you at Tom's Place?'

'Yes, of course Joe,' they all replied together. They left, slamming the door behind them. In the now quiet little factory, Ernie and old Joseph stood together in the middle of a lot of packages and labels.

'Well,' stuttered Ernie, surprise on his face, 'Tom's Place will have full employment next week, whoever Tom is.'

'Tom's Place is a little cafe in the high street,' explained Joseph, we meet there every Saturday for lunch, it's cheap and cheerful. We have a chat over a burger. We're friends you see, apart from working together, we're friends.'

'Friends,' Ernie smiled a lost smile, 'That's something I haven't got. I haven't got any...'

'...friends,' Joseph finished the sentence for him. 'they're called friends, Ernie. Look, take a seat by this bench for a minute. Let's have a chat, after all, you aint got much else to do have you?' As Ernie sat by the bench, Joseph leaned against the other side and continued to talk.

'I'm going to tell you a story, It's a true story, but I want you to keep it to yourself, a secret. Here we go: when I started Pearsall's Plastic Packaging Limited, I...'

'You started this company?' Ernie cried, 'but your name's Pearson...'

'Well, not really,' continued Joseph, 'it's Pearsall, actually, I just use the Pearson name while I'm here. Anyway, when I started this little company, I did the packaging myself at first, then employed a few people, and it was me! I was the big cheese, the main man, the bigwig. I told people what to do and where to go. And the longer I played the part of the number one guy, the more I was disliked, and the more I disliked myself for being so nasty to people.

'And you know, I slowly, over the years, demoted myself from boss man, to packer, to tea maker, label keeper and order organiser, but mainly "friend", friend to every person in this tiny company, and I now have friends for life, and that's how I like it. . I don't want to pry into your own life Ernie, but I guess, as you say, you don't have any friends, those people you like and they like you. Not people who *have* to do what you say, but people who are with you because they want to be.'

'Well, you know,' Ernie spoke quietly, 'I always wanted to be important, to be the man, the bigwig, and all I've ever got is to be alone.'

'Come to Tom's Place cafe on Saturday,' urged Joseph, 'and make friends with your workforce, they're good people.' Ernie went on Saturday and for the first time in a very long time, sat and ate lunch *in company*.

Three weeks later in the factory of Pearsall's Plastic Packaging Limited, a radio quietly played pop music in the background as the workforce packaged away with Ernie at the first bench. Nearby, Susan Redford stood on her box giving a big smile from beneath her black shiny hair towards the slim young man in the denim jacket and trousers sitting by the wall. It was her son Peter, who nowadays was dropped here from the day centre, where he sat happily reading his magazines. 'Ernie! Ernie,' cried Elaine from her bench, waving her good arm, 'that's twelve packages I've done today.'

'Great, Elaine,' smiled Ernie, 'that's really great, but don't overdo it.'

'Ernie, can I sit on your bike outside at lunch today?' Greg asked eagerly.

'Course you can,' smiled Ernie, 'but be careful, Greg, don't fall off, I can't afford to lose one of my best workers, can I?'

Big Wig

Wigs have been known since the time of the ancient Egyptians. In England by the mid-seventeenth century wigs were highly fashionable. They were also extremely expensive, so the most successful of men would buy the most expensive wig, showing off their substantial wealth. The bigger the wig, the more powerful and rich was the wearer. Samuel Pepys, the famous London diarist, bought a wig in the sixteen sixties and was a fashionable success, and as he grew in wealth and power, so he bought a bigger wig. He was a bigwig.

THE CLOAK

Alexander Hurley shifted the weight of his backpack and trudged into the empty railway station and touched-in his travel card. At ten o'clock on a summer Saturday night it was finally getting really dark as the homeward bound night traffic sped by on the busy main road outside the station. Alexander looked up at the display board and sighed, the next train for the city was going to be over an hour before it got here. Alexander was quite tall and thin, and looked older than his twenty-eight years, with his thin light brown hair, dark tanned face with thick eyebrows over brown eyes and shortish nose, with stubble round his long chin with its set mouth. He wore his usual denim shirt with rolled up sleeves and three-quarter denim shorts and black trainers. The small station had no staff, a rusty coffee machine, a cash money dispenser, and not much else. He ambled down the darkening platform until he came to a bench where one young man sat, looking intensely at the screen of his mobile phone.

'Hi,' Alexander mumbled as he slipped out of his backpack and sat next to the young man. The young feller looked up briefly, then went back to his phone. He had dark hair brushed back, a squarish face with wide mouth and clean shaven chin. He wore a white shirt with blue tie and a dark blue suit with black leather shoes. The two sat in silence for a moment, the young man still looking seriously at his phone, while Alexander stared up and down the empty train platform.

'Goin' into the city?' Alexander asked.

'Hmm?' the young man raised his head, dragging his eyes away from his phone, 'oh, oh, yeah.' Then his head bent down as he resumed his intent reading of his mobile.

'Been visiting? Going to work?' Alexander asked of the stranger.

'What? No... I...' the young man sighed and put his phone in his pocket, he'd have to catch up on looking at his mobile later, this guy, this total stranger, wanted to talk. 'Oh well,' he answered, 'it's a long time till the train gets here so, no, I'm not visiting, I'm going home, I've been visiting my mum, just ordinary visiting, my name's Kenny, Kenny Smith.'

'Hi, I'm Alexander,' Alexander settled back on the bench, 'and I wish my life was ordinary, it was ordinary once and I really wish it was ordinary now.'

'Wow, you must have had some bad luck,' Kenny asked, secretly wishing he was alone again.

'Bad luck. Yeah, I s'pose you *could* call it that,' continued Alexander, 'see, me and a pal found a reference to a book, written by a guy called Geoffrey of Monmouth, which was written in the twelfth century. It's called the *Historia regum Britanniae* which means the History of the Kings of Britain, but it's all about King Arthur, his castle called Camelot, his cloak of invisibility and the devious magician Merlin and the magic sword Excalibur which Arthur pulled from a large stone to prove he was the true King, and then defeating the Saxon invaders.'

'Well, I'm sure it was all very interesting,' interrupted Kenny, 'but how did it bring you a bad time?'

'Well, I really got into it,' explained Alexander, 'finding out about the Knights of the Round Table, which is where King Arthur's knights met, and their chivalrous deeds. So I *had* to go to the famous castle of Camelot, it's in South Wales. As I was absolutely skint and unemployed at the time, I hitched my way there, and when I saw the ruins of the once great castle, I could imagine all the knights there with their shining armour and swirling, colourful capes. I wandered the ruins of the castle until late at night, and eventually slept at the bottom of a great wall of the building.

'During the night, it became quite chilly and the wind was whistling through the open walls, and I began to hear a sound like men's voices, giving orders and calling others to battle. So I dragged myself up and, pulling my backpack on, began searching the castle grounds for the ghosts of Arthur's knights or magician's casting spells. I wandered round the massive walls and somehow stumbled and fell into a deep trench of some sort. I was winded as I landed on a hard floor in the fall and looked further into the trench, where I could see an opening in the earth! And something seemed to glitter in the shadowy darkness inside.

'I wriggled through and found myself in a large, dark, cave-like place where rusty chain links and old metal parts lay about the ground, and there! A small wooden box, covered in dust. It had a tiny label on the lid when I brushed and blew away the thick dust, which pronounced in old English: "Mantle of Invisibility". It was said that one of King Arthur's prized possessions was his cloak of invisibility, and I had found it! If the cloak was in the box, I could become invisible.

'I grabbed the box and wriggled out of there, stuffed the box into my backpack and started walking. By the time the morning light had come, I was tired, cold and hungry, walking along a lonely country road. I kept thumbing, trying to get a lift, every time a vehicle passed, with no luck, until eventually, I sat outside a long deserted roadside cafe, where tourists would stop for tea and cakes, maybe still did in the summer season. As I sat on a rickety chair, I fiddled with the box and prised it open. I couldn't see anything inside, but I could feel some sort of fabric. I pulled it out and tugged it over myself, it covered my head, down to the tops of my legs. I stood and looked in my reflection in the dusty tea room window. I was not there! But I *was* there! I went close to the window, and there was no reflection of me. I was invisible.'

'You were invisible,' Kenny asked in surprise, 'so how did that bring you bad luck?'

'Well, my first deed with the cloak of invisibility,' sighed Alexander, 'happened later that day when a truck pulled up and the driver offered to drop me off at the next town. On the drive I told him that if he bought me a full breakfast at the next cafe, when we got into the next town, I'd draw sixty quid out of the hole in the wall and give it all to him. Well, I can tell you, at that cafe, I had the full monty! Jumbo cooked breakfast, with coffee and toast. When, later, we pulled up at the ATM in the next town, as the driver got out of his side of the truck and walked round to my side, I pulled on the cloak. You should have seen his face when he looked into the passenger side of the cab! He couldn't see me! His jaw dropped and he looked round all sides of the pavement, the truck's cab, and underneath, then scratched his head as I walked away.

'Then I wandered into a large supermarket where I donned the cloak again and leant over a girl at the checkout and took all the banknotes in the till. The money I took paid for a travel card and a night in a hostel.

'In the next town I put on the cloak and went into the art museum where I mixed up all the famous paintings on the walls just to watch the security guards run round like frightened rabbits, that's when I learned to keep out of the way of running people, if they can't see you they can't move out of your way, I nearly got knocked over a couple of times.

'Travelling on, each day I took from checkout tills, sneaked in behind a bank worker into the back of a bank and took rolls of notes; walked out - unseen of course - of hotels without paying, had meals in restaurants, took taxi's, and did just what I liked, you see, hiding in full view of people who can't see you is a great thrill on its own that is so addictive.

'But now, well, you know, I'm absolutely ashamed of myself, all I've done with this wonderful gift of invisibility is to turn to crime and deception.'

'Think of what you could have done,' Kenny was aghast, 'you could have worked for the Government, seeing what other countries are up to, kept watch of gangs of villains for the police, watched over prisons and terrorist groups...'

'Yes, you're right,' sighed Alexander, 'I've decided. One more job, to set me up with enough money to get home, and I'm giving it all up...'

'What you gonna do?' Kenny looked shocked, 'rob someone else? How much do you need?'

' 'bout three hundred quid. I'll just take some till money somewhere...'

'Hold on. Hold on,' Kenny held his hands up, palms forward, 'I'm listening to you, but come to think of it, it just sounds a bit iffy to me.'

'Wanna see it?' Alexander asked, pulling out his backpack. He rummaged inside for a few moments, then pulled out a small black bag with a pull-string top. He tugged at the strings, opened the bag and turned it towards Kenny, who peered inside.

'It's empty,' Kenny said flatly, looking up at Alexander with suspicious eyes, 'there's nothing in there.'

'Course it's not empty,' answered Alexander, 'it's in there alright.'

'I can't see a thing in there,' Kenny again looked accusingly at Alexander.

'Well, of course you can't see it,' smiled Alexander, 'it's invisible.' Kenny stared into the bag. Alexander gently pulled *something* out of the bag and slowly wriggled it over Kenny's head and shoulders.

'I can't see it,' Kenny said questioningly, 'but I can see me,' he said as he raised his arm, hand in front of his face.

'Hey! Hey!' Alexander shouted, 'don't run off with my cloak! Where are you? I can't see you!'

'Of course you can see me,' laughed Kenny nervously, 'I'm right here, in front of you.' But still Alexander was looking this way and that, eyes wide, and only jerked to a stop when Kenny gripped his arm.

'Well, I can't see you,' Alexander answered, 'look! Look! A young girl has just walked onto the platform, waiting for the same train as us, I reckon. Go up to her, talk to her, see if she can see you or not, that'll be proof that you're really wearing the cloak of invisibility.'

Kenny marched along the platform to where the new arrival stood. The girl had long brown hair, dark eyes in a dusky skin, white teeth and red lipsticked lips, she wore a light coloured long water proof coat, black stockings and high heeled shiny shoes. 'Scuse me, love,' Kenny stammered, 'I know this may sound like a silly chat up line, but can you see me? Am I invisible?' The girl looked away with a jerk of her head, nose in the air. Kenny ran back down the platform to Alexander. 'It works. It works; she couldn't see me. Look, take your cloak back for a moment. And you said three hundred quid would get you your new start? I'll go to the cash machine and get you your money.' Alexander slowly, unfeelingly peeled the *something* from Kenny's head and folded it away in the little black bag, pulling the strings together tightly.

Kenny came back from the cash machine and gave Alexander the three hundred quid in exchange for the little black bag.

Suddenly the train thundered down into the station, filling the platform with light and noise. Alexander took up his backpack and walked smartly to the front of the train, leaving Kenny to enter a different carriage.

Some twenty minutes later, the train pulled in at the next stop. Only Alexander got out of the train, which soon left, leaving the platform a lonely litter-strewn place. Within a few minutes a young man entered the station, touched in with his travel card, looked at the arrivals board and sighed; the next train was going to be an hour's wait. He pulled his mobile phone from his pocket and began to leaf through...

'Goin' into the city?' someone asked.

'Hmm?' the young man raised his head, 'Oh, yeah, you know, just the usual thing...'

'Hi, I'm Alexander,' the new person said as he settled back on the bench, 'and I wish my life was "the usual", it was usual once and I really wish it was usual now.'

'Well, you must have had a bad time,' the young man said, secretly wishing he was alone again.

'Bad time. Yeah, I s'pose you *could* call it that,' continued Alexander, 'see, me and a pal found a reference to a book, written by a guy called Geoffrey of Monmouth written in the twelfth century...'

SOME STORY

As the American professional gamblers used to say in the nineteenth century, when fleecing visitors on their gambling tables: "There's one born every minute". And didn't a famous American comic say there was a sucker born every minute?

KING

'This morning, we could make history,' Katherine Bayliss said quietly, almost to herself as she looked at the shadowy figure of the tiny, throbbing, furry little body inside its mother's womb. The picture she watched showed clearly the inside of the female wolf's body on a large screen, above the anaesthetised animal. The operating table was on the lab top of the white tiled laboratory. Katherine summed up the story so far:

'When I was on the Seaforth University's visit to North America and Canada where we found those frozen pre-historic wolf remains, I just had to save the spermatozoa from the animal, which had lain in the permafrost for thousands and thousands of years.'

'And now, we've mixed that with the eggs of a modern North American wolf,' said Harvey Mayall, standing by her side, looking at the screen with interest, 'we are going to give birth, through a surrogate mother, to the first wild wolf in this country for a very very, long time.'

Katherine Bayliss was twenty five years old, with shortish blond hair, tied tightly at the back of her tanned face, with her dark eyebrows, brown eyes, thin nose and wide smile showing her even, white teeth. She wore the standard white lab coat over a white, square necked dress which just covered her knees, and pink high heeled shoes. Harvey Mayall was just a little older, black, with shaven head, deep brown eyes, a wide smile and a thin stubbly beard, wearing a blue shirt under his white coat, with blue jeans and soft brown shoes.

Together the two had shown great interest in the test tube birth of babies and of animals, and now since Katherine's visit to the frozen far north and her taking of the spermatozoa, they had rejuvenated the tiny particles that they had got and fertilized them in a petri dish with the father's sperm, and introduced them into a modern female wolf's womb. And now the tiny baby wolf was actually wrestling with new life in the mother's body. The minuscule animal, still wet, was squirming as they released it from the parent and injected a small amount of energy giving liquid into its tiny body system.

'When this little fellah makes his first appearance in the national newspapers and TV,' grinned Harvey, as he watched their creation move it's tiny rat-like legs on its scrawny, glistening-wet body, 'we'll be the most famous research students in Seaforth University's history.

'I think I'll call him King,' smiled Katherine, 'the king of the next generation of wolves.' The two smiled as they left the laboratory.

Two hours later, and the pair returned, eager to see how their creation was getting on. Both stood before the glass on the lab top and stared at it in disbelief. 'He's not moving,' Katherine whispered, her voiced trailing off.

'He's dead.' Harvey said flatly, 'look; all the monitor screens are flat lining.'

'How horrible,' Katherine's eyes were filled with tears as she opened the glass front and plucked the tiny, limp body from the tray, 'poor little King.' She held the little creature in the palm of her hand and looked down at him.

'Come on,' Harvey soothed, 'we tried. Let him go. Perhaps it was not to be, a pre-historic creature born again.' He gently lifted the tiny body from Katherine's hand and laid it by the "non-recycle" bin, where it would be picked up later and taken to the incinerator. Harvey put his arm around Katherine's shoulders and together they sadly left the laboratory.

Time passed and King's body shone and glistened less; he began to dry out. His whole fifty millimetre long body gave a great lurch as water from his liquid-filled lungs gushed from his mouth and nose in one go. This convulsion turned King over as he drew his first ever breath and landed him just beneath a powerful lamp which shone down fiercely on him.

For the next few hours, the tiny creature's body was pumped with oxygen and heat beneath the hot light, gaining strength with each moment.

Suddenly the laboratory door was opened as someone walked in, then slammed the door closed behind them. The noise – the first sound King had ever heard – made him jump and he twisted and rolled off the lab top. The little new-born animal slid down the side of the soft plastic sack that was the "non-recycle" bag and landed gently on the floor. Instinctively he scurried into a corner for safety, opening his eyes for the first time, but he was still too young to be able to see. He waited patiently.

King was soon forgotten in the laboratory, as Harvey and Katherine believed his little body had been taken for the incinerator, and they had moved on to the next project. King squeezed into his corner beneath the lab tops and drank from spilt water and ate crumbs. Then one morning, he opened his eyes and found that he could see! By now about the size of a mouse, he soon learned to move around after dark, and to secretly enter and exit rooms at the same time as the cleaning staff who wedged doors open.

King's hearing was acute, his sense of smell like radar, his new found eyesight sharp and clear. As night fell in the laboratories, he prowled for food, finding leftovers, dregs of coffee and tea and tearing to pieces any tiny animals he came across; spiders, beetles and bugs; he ripped them apart, sometimes to eat and sometimes because he was a hunter.

When one night, he finally arrived down at the ground floor and made his way outside, he was strong, powerful and the size of a fully grown cat. As he stepped onto the grass of the Seaforth University's green park land, with its tall trees, that surrounded the campus buildings, his senses soared. To be outside, in the open! The sharp air, the smell of the grass and woodland; the scent of animals, all filled him with energy.

His fur was jet black on his back and lighter brown down by his strong legs, and his tail was long and swishing. Sniff! What was that scent? His black eyes narrowed as his nose twitched this way and that to identify where the smell was coming from. His large canine teeth showed strong, white and hungry as his lips curled back in anticipation of a kill.

In the darkness, under a thick bush, tucked well out of sight, he found it. A wood pigeon had trapped itself, being caught by its claws on the exposed roots of a bush. The bird turned in terror as King slid mercilessly under the foliage. The bird squarked and screeched, trying to tear itself away. King lunged and ripped off its head. He ate well that night.

Amid the blood soaked feathers and bones of the wood pigeon, King made his new home under this bush. He kept out of the way of the students and staff of the University during the day and hunted at night, when it was quiet. He stalked the campus park land and grew. He was soon a full sized wolf.

King's hunting area was the ground surrounding the University buildings, but the best food was to be had on the other side of the strip of road that ran through the middle of the park land. This was where the student's and visitors held their barbecues on the warmer evenings and left juicy food behind for him to eat, and attack and kill the foxes who came to steal what he had claimed. But King had to be careful, he didn't understand roads and traffic, but soon learnt that the wheeled vehicles that sped along its smooth-surface through the park could hurt him if he got in the way, so he kept away until it was dark, and not so busy, and he could see and dodge approaching headlights.

As time passed, he became bigger and stronger, wiser in the ways of man; he could lie perfectly still, his black furred body hidden in shadows, watching as people ate their sandwiches, pies, chicken, and sugary doughnuts and then left their rubbish on the ground near the heat of the barbecue embers, pack themselves into the car, and drive off. Then he would run across the tarmac road and help himself to the leftovers, and afterwards chase down and kill a lurking fox, just for fun.

One early evening as night was falling, King watched from across the tarmac. Three adults cooked at a barbecue for a gang of children. Lots of fizzy drinks and chicken bits. King's eyes narrowed as he watched the noisy kids. Some of the younger ones were very, very small.

As the night drew in with a chill in the air, the humans packed up ready to leave. King edged forward, saliva dribbling from his mouth between long, strong teeth. The people took their rubbish, packed it into plastic bags, threw the bags onto the ground near the overflowing waste bins and began to load the kids into their nearby car. Soon they were ready to drive off, the children waving out of the open windows of the car. But what was this? One small child, a little girl with long brown curly hair, in a short sleeved long dress and red trainers, slid out of the car window, dropped to the floor and ran around the smouldering debris of the barbecue, a hand to her mouth to hide her mischievous grin as she hid from the adults in the car.

The vehicle drove off across the grass, but then after a hundred or so metres, the car skidded to a halt as the adults discovered there was a missing child. The little girl shrieked with laughter and ran into the woods beyond the picnic area.

King's head jerked up. This was his chance. He could race into the woods, catch the child in his great teeth, crunch down to silence the little one, and run off, way before the adults had even scoured the barbecue area to find her gone.

King sprang from his shaded cover to the road, and raced across the tarmac. Crunch! The thirty-eight ton truck smashed into him, killing him instantly, crushing his body at forty miles per hour, then smashing it into the hard tarmac surface with its many trailer tyres. 'Bloomin' foxes.' The driver said as he felt the impact. 'Bloomin' foxes.' He didn't stop.

The adults found the little girl, still giggling, near the trees surrounding the picnic area.

Jump the gun

To do something without thinking first. To make a sudden and unexpected movement. In athletics, to start the race before the starting gun has gone off.

THE NEWGATE BELL

In a dim stone-walled alley way behind the London church of Saint Sepulchre, a man appeared. He was about thirty years old, tall, with long brown hair brushed straight downwards at the sides and back, had thin eyebrows over brown eyes, with a short nose, nervous smile and squarish teeth, and he was clean shaven with just a hint of stubble on his chin. He wore a grey woollen cap, a blue laced-up tunic with long sleeves, three quarter-length light brown trousers, long stockings and buckled black leather shoes.

His name was William Vaugrenard, and he was nervous because when he appeared in the alley behind the church, he had become the world's first time traveller. He had travelled from the late twenty-first century to here, the middle of the seventeenth century, in fact the exact year was 1650, and he was dressed in the costume of the day.

William Vaugrenard had been a research scientist for the Kaylor Research and Development Company for a long time. He had been working on FTL - faster than light technology - and had actually managed to send atomic particles into the future. Everyone knows that the speed of light is as fast as anything can travel, but like many scientists William knew better. If you can send an atomic particle faster than 186,000 miles per second, which is the speed of light, then that particle is travelling in time.

William had worked on the problem for the last six years, and had developed a particle accelerator which could take a man into the future or the past. It was his experiment, his baby, and the bosses at Kaylor R&D had let him decide where he, the first time traveller, should go.

William took a couple of days off from the rigours of his scientific work before his historic trip into another time. On one particular day, he and his wife had taken a day trip to London. When they strolled across Holborn Viaduct they came upon the church of Saint Sepulchre, one of the biggest and oldest churches in central London. Its actual name is Saint Sepulchre-without-Newgate as it is situated just outside of the old city of London walls, and has a very strange part in history.

The church is placed just opposite the Old Bailey courthouse, which was once the site of the most notorious prison in London: Newgate. The old Newgate prison was dark, unclean, full of lice and creepy-crawlies, and many deadly human diseases, and was also infamous for its cruelty to its prisoners, who were fed on scraps of food and water, sometimes beaten and often left chained to the cell walls.

In the church of Saint Sepulchre is a hand bell – it is still there – and on the night before a public execution – the bell would be rung by a church official as he walked down a tunnel which connected the church across the road to Newgate prison, where the bell would only stop ringing when the church man was outside the cell of the condemned prisoner. All the way on the journey through the tunnel, the churchman would chant:

"All you that in the condemned hold do lie,
Prepare you, for to-morrow you shall die;
Watch all, and pray, the hour is drawing near,
That you before the Almighty must appear;
Examine well yourselves, in time repent,
That you may not to eternal flames be sent.
And when St. Sepulchre's bell to-morrow tolls,
The Lord above have mercy on your souls.
Past twelve o'clock!"

Then the prisoner would be led down the ever-narrowing Dead Man's Walk, where the ceiling and the walls get narrower, like a corridor in a nightmare, making the prisoner easier to control, should he throw a panic and try to escape.

William read of this strange ritual with the bell and then by chance came across a list of some of the prisoners who were held in the old condemned cells at Newgate. He read:

John Cooke — prosecutor of Charles I
George Barrington — pickpocket
Claude Du Vall — highwayman
Moll Cutpurse — pickpocket and fence
James MacLaine — highwayman
William Vaugrenard — anarchist

'Wow, that's my name!' William Vaugrenard cried as he read the last name. 'I mean, there's only a few people with the name Vaugrenard in this country, anyway. How strange.' It was unusual, but not impossible, someone all those years ago had the same name as him. But it intrigued him, and when the time came for him to try the time travel experiment at the Kaylor laboratories, he knew when he would be travelling to. He would just have to go see who his namesake was. A family ancestor? Was he a direct descendant? He just had to know. He did some research and found that William Vaugrenard the anarchist was executed in the year 1650.

And now here he was, in 1650, outside the church of Saint Sepulchre a few days before the anarchist Vaugrenard was to be executed. He walked to the end of the alley and out into the sunshine of seventeenth century London. As he walked he looked back into the alley, to remember it well. He had to be back in four hours, in the exact spot where he had landed in this time. That was when the atomic collider that brought him here would reverse and take him back to his own era. He checked the time on his digital pocket watch, then tucked it back into his pocket. He was dressed in the costume of the time, but if anyone saw his watch, it would seem strange, as watches were extremely rare at this time, and a digital watch was many hundreds of years in the future.

He was now out in a narrow lane, which had a surface made of rounded stones packed together and the buildings on either side were made of a white painted smooth substance with exposed wooden beams. Each storey of the houses and shops were overhanging the level below, and most of the roofs were thatched or tiled with slates. The lane was very noisy with the sound of much talking and shouting. Litter and animal pooh was strewn across the street and there seemed to be a million flies in the air. Men, mainly dressed like William in woolly hats and drab clothes shuffled by or drove small herds of animals to and from markets, while women wearing cloth scarves on their heads, long sleeved woollen tops and long dresses which reached to the ankles where leather slippers were worn.

In the busy street, cattle mooed, pigs grunted and clucking ducks and geese were all herded along. In the shops, men wearing aprons over their clothes called out their wares, asking the passing men and women to enter their workplace to buy goods.

As he walked on, he headed in the direction of the prison of Newgate; it was difficult to tell the actual route to follow as at this date, there were many different streets and houses which were not still standing in the modern era, especially after the great fire of London, when so much of the city was burnt to the ground.

Outside some of the shops and businesses that he passed, animal carcasses hung, and wooden tables and stools stood outside taverns and eating establishments, where people were sitting, drinking and eating. None of the shops had written signs above, but many had painted symbols to show the passing, mainly illiterate, population what they sold.

William walked through the rising murk and dust to where he hoped the infamous prison was situated. The sounds of the city were almost as loud as the noise of his day, without machinery or cars, what with the animals and people crowding into the narrow roads and lanes.

Then he turned a corner and saw it, it had to be: a massive, dark, stone-built long building, three storeys high and three hundred metres long with small barred windows. A raised wooden staircase went from the street level up to a large open wooden door where two uniformed guards stood. William warily climbed to the top of the staircase.

At the top of the stairs, the guards stood in his way. They both wore a black uniform of woollen cap, long sleeved jacket with coat tails, long trousers and black boots. Both had unruly hair protruding from beneath their caps, dirty faces and unfriendly scowls. One carried a ring of large keys, the other held a length of chain. 'What do you want?' one demanded of him.

'Oh, well...' stammered William, 'I'd like to visit a prisoner if I may?'

'What's 'is name?' demanded the guard on the left.

'What's 'e done?' asked the other, 'why's 'e in here?'

'Anarchy, I believe,' explained William, 'I can pay you for this visit...' he didn't get the chance to offer the money he had brought with him, taken from a private collection of old coins, as the two guards jumped at him, the first one wrapping the short chain round his hands and the second grabbing him around the neck. They marched him into the prison, stifling his protestations and bustling him along.

The guards bundled William through a dim, stone-walled passageway, passing many closed doors. At the end of the passage, they burst through double wooden doors into a courtroom with dirty narrow windows high in the walls. It had a raised wooden public gallery at one end and a judges high desk at the other; both were made of faded old dark wood, which was patched and boarded up. The high ceiling of the courtroom was dark with many years of dust and dirt, matching its windows with accumulated grime. The public gallery was full of squabbling and arguing people: the men in three pointed hats, long scruffy powdered wigs and old long sleeved jackets with knee breeches, stockings and buckled shoes, the women wore thick yellow make up and wore large hats, shawls and long dresses, all seemed to be talking at the same time.

Then William was bundled into a booth with a guard on each side of him, where he was facing an old man at the far end of the court, sitting at the high judges desk, peering over the top, wearing a long white wig which seemed to cover half of his old, lined, face, while around his shoulders was wound the top end of a worn cloak. The old man at the desk looked up with a bored expression. 'What's he here for?' he demanded, ruffling the papers and inkwell on the desk top before him.

'He's an Anarchist, Judge.' announced one of the guards at William's side, 'he says he's an anarchist, come here to visit a friend, an inmate.' The noisy jabbering of the crowd in the public gallery stopped into complete silence as the people stared at William in disbelief.

'Anarchist, eh?' the judge grabbed a large quill pen from the desk top, dipped it quickly into the ink pot and began to scribble notes on a paper in front of him. 'What's your name?' he demanded of William.

'Vaugrenard...' At the sound of his name the crowd "oohhed" and "aarrghed".

'Vaugrenard! A Frenchman.' the judge stared at William with a withering glare. 'We've been at war with France as long as I can remember. What's an enemy Frenchman doing here?'

'No, no,' insisted William, I'm a Londoner, not a Frenchman, when I found my way here to see my kinsman...'

'*Found* your way here?' the judge hooted at William amid calls and shouts from the near rioting crowd, 'Londoner's don't have to find their way here, to *Newgate*.' The judge pointed a bony finger at William, 'everyone knows Newgate prison!'

'No, no, I *am* from London, just not quite, now... You see,' William tried to explain above the crowd's shouting, 'the streets will change because there's going to be a fire, a big fire, the whole of London will burn to the ground...'

'A fire?' the judge roared, 'a fire! Your here to get your kinsman out of Newgate prison and set fire to London?' The public gallery was now in uproar, with shouts of 'Hang him!' 'Put him on the rack to make him talk!'

'No... no.' William shouted to be heard, 'I'm from another... time. Another place.' Look! Look,' he said as he pulled from his pocket his digital timepiece and gave it to one of the guards. The guard took the timepiece from him and held it as if it might blow up. He ran across the courtroom and threw it onto the judge's desk.

'It... it's got numbers dancing across it!' the judge screamed as he brushed it off his desk top with a big swipe. The small digital watch flew over the courtroom into the public gallery where the crowd screamed and ran into each other as they escaped from the room in dire panic, as they waited for it to explode.

One of the guards retrieved the watch; it was broken. 'Take him down.' ordered the judge and William was bundled down into a line of filthy cells where he was chained to the wall.

Time passed, well after the time for the collider to reverse and take William back to his own time. Would his employers at Kaylor send someone to save him? *Could* they send someone here to save him? How would they locate him? Where would they go to find him, if they could get here?

Days passed, no-one spoke to William. Stale bread and rancid water were shoved under the cage door of his cell, which he could just reach.

Weeks passed in absolute loneliness for William, just the occasional guard would pass him by and mutter: 'Anarchist!'

Then one night he heard that chant, the one that came from the church of Saint Sepulchre's. The ringing of the bell and the chant got closer and closer, and finally stopped at his cell door:

"And when St. Sepulchre's bell to-morrow tolls,
The Lord above have mercy on your souls.
Past twelve o'clock!"

So now he knew; the William Vaugrenard he had read about, the anarchist held in Newgate prison was *him!*

Look before you leap

Look before you leap. Check that you are clear what is ahead of you before making a decision that you cannot go back on.

This proverb may derive from the undeniable wisdom of checking a fence before jumping over it on horseback, or not leaping into marriage without being absolutely sure.

The actual Newgate Execution Bell
is on perpetual display in the
church of St Sepulchre in London

TROY STORY

The jet black Buell City X v-twin motor cycle roared along the traffic-filled city street. The rider, Troy Addison, twisted the hand grip as hard as it would go and the 984cc engine responded with great power as rider and bike thundered along the dotted line in the middle of the crowded two-way road. Troy grinned to himself inside his matt black crash helmet as the drivers of the cars and vans coming towards him swore at him and shook their fists as he flew towards them, headlights blazing.

Troy was in his early twenties, fairly short with a strong wiry body, bright brown eyes beneath short-cropped dark hair, with smooth skin, stubby nose and cheekily grinning mouth showing gappy teeth.

Troy loved his job - he was self-employed! he was his own boss - he had worked hard setting it up by himself; he had bought the bike, leather outfit and crash helmet, paid big insurance premiums, including GIT – Goods In Transit – which was double the normal insurance. Then he had paid many smiling visits to different offices in the city, ensuring them of his super fast efficiency in delivering goods and paperwork in quick time.

Eventually he had convinced about half a dozen city offices to use him as their courier, for his clients were very important to him, because if he had no contacts he had no work. So now, when he was contacted – his telephone was wired directly into his crash helmet – he would flit from one office building, pick up paperwork and deliver to another office or bank, or restaurant, takeaway, or florist, anything that he could do for his clients.

And of course, he was the best. He was the fastest round the city streets, he knew every road, alley, park and walkway where his bike would fit, he would nip up one way streets the wrong way, jump the lights and cross pavements. Most of all, he enjoyed being the fastest and best despatch rider around. Troy loved whizzing up and down the busy city thoroughfares.

At this moment, after turning off the main road, he was flying down a narrow road: an office bosses' forgotten mobile phone in his extra large back pack. He had to get to the bank on Fletcher Street to get the man his phone. He swerved to the right of a slowing taxi, right into the path of an oncoming van. The driver pulled sharply to his left and Troy just got round in time. 'Wow,' cried Troy, 'now, that was close!' When he turned in from the oncoming van, he had looked right into the eyes of the enraged driver.

He accelerated out in front of the traffic into the main, busy road of Oldbench Road, then turned quickly into Fletcher Street, followed by much hooting of motorists behind him. He roared up to the bank, jumped off his bike, ran up the stairs to the counter where Mr Finch, the office boss, waited for his forgotten mobile. Troy raised his helmet and gave a theatrical bow, then passed the phone to the man. 'Well done, Troy,' the boss man said as he took his phone and walked on to his meeting.

As Troy reached his bike outside the bank, he switched on his phone and started his engine, at the same time noticing a rather plump and sweaty black-with-yellow-stripes uniformed traffic warden making his hasty way towards Troy's bike, which had been standing on double yellow lines. The approaching traffic warden, an older man, seemed out-of-breath and unfit to waddle very fast, with a puffy red face, his peaked cap on the back of his sweating head, with dangly, stringy dark hair, troubled dark eyes and with an unshaven, stubbly chin. Troy stamped on the gear pedal and roared away, before the warden could get close enough to see his registration plate. Troy tap danced on the gear pedal to take him out of there at maximum speed.

'Hi, Troy,' a voice spoke into his ear through his phone, 'Don Petersen here, at Bronson's Head Office. Would you pick up some flowers for me at Trott's Florist on Headley Street, and get them to this office a-s-a-p? It's my anniversary and the wife's coming for lunch. Can you get here in about ten minutes?'

'Sure.' answered Troy as he slammed on his brakes and swung sharply right, across surprised traffic coming towards him, and dived into a tiny alley between some shops, and blasted down the middle, swerving between shoppers. He arrived at Trott's Florist shop, slid off the bike and walked quickly through the open shop door. 'Flowers for Mister Petersen?' Troy asked. A young girl assistant gave Troy the flowers which he slipped in his back pack and went outside to his bike. Starting up the bike, selecting first gear and twisting the grip to roar away, Troy saw once again the sweaty, red faced, plump traffic warden treading hard towards him. He raced quickly off.

'Hello, Troy?' another voice spoke in his ear.

'Yoh!' Troy called back into his helmet microphone as he raced through the gears and zoomed around the traffic jams towards Bronson's Head Office.

'Troy, it's Pete Russell here, from The Nurses Agency,' the phone buzzed on, 'can you get to the council offices and pick up some passports for me? D'you think you get over there in about fifteen minutes?'

'Be there in twelve minutes,' Troy grinned to himself. This was going to be tricky, from his next delivery at Bronson's Head Office, the council offices were on the other side of the park, a good ten minute ride at full pelt. Then he had the answer! He'd go through the park!

Soon he zoomed right up to the swing doors of Bronson's Head Office, jumped off his bike, ran in and put the flowers on the reception desk. 'Flowers for Mister Petersen,' he addressed the smart young lady at the desk with her flowing black hair, dark eyebrows and red lips, her white blouse and painted nails the only view of her at the desk.

'No crash helmet's allowed in here,' she smirked, 'Anyway, you'll have to wait. I'll have to see if I can contact him.'

'No, love, I'm not waiting,' Troy laughed out loud, 'believe me, he'll be relieved to accept these flowers.' "Funny", he thought, "how some people hate despatch riders, even more than motorists do." He turned, left the reception, and vaulted back on his bike, just in time to once more just miss the flustered looking tubby traffic warden as he rounded the corner and waddled towards Troy. He gunned his engined and escaped.

He raced through the traffic and turned into the park, right in front of a large lorry which was thundering towards him. 'Wow!' he thought, 'that was another close one!' He hammered through the park, making sure he didn't scare some little kid in his path; he knew he shouldn't be in here on a motor bike. And then – Oh no! - a school trip of tiny kids being herded along the path by a couple of teachers. The kids filled the pathway before him as he roared along. He turned off the tarmac path onto the grass and sped over a hill. In the distance, across at the other side of the green, he could see the iron gates at the other end of the park.

He sped passed some people sitting on the grass, upsetting their small dog who took chase after Troy's bike and had to be brought back by the angry family.

At the park gates he looked to his right and gauged the distance between two oncoming cars. He flew out of the gate between the cars and had only a half metre between him and the second car, causing the driver to blast on his horn. Troy boosted away by dropping a gear and giving it full power. As he thundered on, he thought: "I'm glad I've got this tight fitting leather suit on, if I had been wearing a loose coat, that car could have caught me."

Troy skidded to a stop at the council offices where he had to park his bike in the motorcycle parking area, this had to be done correctly as the council had CCTV and would fine any biker who parked wrongly. He ran into the office and found that the passports were ready and in a large envelope, waiting for him to sign for them. After a few moments stuffing the envelope into his back pack, Troy was out astride his bike again.

He swung his back pack through his arms and onto his back, started up and jamming his foot on the gear pedal, raced off. Just as he sped away, he thought he caught a glimpse of a tubby sort of bloke in a yellow peaked cap, red sweaty face and traffic warden's uniform. Was this guy after giving him a ticket, or did they have a lot of tubby look-alike wardens?

He left the oncoming warden in a cloud of exhaust smoke and tyre rubber, and roared into the traffic, making his way to The Nurses Agency, just a few short streets away. He raced through the traffic, then remembered that his quickest route to the Nurses Agency was the next turning left, which he was almost level with. He spun left into the bus lane – and woah! - he had turned into the path of an oncoming bus! He jerked his handlebars right and lay over real deep, his knee scraping the ground. The bus was almost on top of him when he straightened up and twisting the throttle, belted away. The bus driver gave a horrified look as he thought that the bike could have gone under his wheels.

Then he was into the nurses agency street, and Troy noticed that the road was grid-locked, at a stand still; traffic both ways had stopped. He aimed his front wheel at the nearest kerb and bumped up. Standing high on the pedals of his bike, he stood tall in the saddle and looking over the heads of the many pedestrians, carved a way down the busy city pavement. Many of the people on the pavement were angry with him, having to jump out of the way and one old lady swung her umbrella at him.

He slid into the tiny car park at the Nurses Agency and stopped, took off his crash helmet, and ran into the entrance as he looked at his watch. 'Made it in twelve minutes!' he announced triumphantly to himself.

Moments later he was back in the saddle and riding off again, back into the busy city traffic. He approached a set of traffic lights; they were at green. 'Hello, that you Troy?' someone said on his helmet phone speaker.

'Yeah?' answered Troy, 'who's that?' he spoke as the lights turned amber.

'Dave Prentiss at City Bank,' came the answer, 'can you do a quick delivery for us?'

'Sure. Be there in a few minutes.' He gunned the bike's engine as the lights went red. Troy thundered over the just-turned-red lights. Crump! He smacked into the side of a lorry going over the lights across in front of him, his face slapping into the metal of the truck body with a loud crack! as his body thudded into the unforgiving metal side. He flew off the bike arms and legs waving helplessly about and crashed! on to the ground with a deep crunching sound, sliding along the hard, gritty ground for seven metres, as he rolled over and over.

He stood up. The world was suddenly extremely quiet. White, hazy smoke billowed around. Troy looked down at his leather clad body to see if he had hurt himself or torn his clothes. No. He was unhurt and his clothing was not ripped.

Troy looked up in surprise as he saw the plump sweaty uniformed traffic warden appear in the mist. 'Oh... it's you.' Troy said in a shaky voice.

'Yes,' smiled the tubby one, 'I knew I'd catch up with you sometime today.'

'Oh... You reckon I'll get nicked or be fined after this accident?' Troy asked.

'No... Not this time Troy.' The warden smiled yet again. Troy noticed that the lorry had disappeared, as had the tarmacked road surface, and the mist was thickening. 'No Troy,' the warden continued, 'this time you were just taking that one chance too many. Come on, son.' The two strolled off into the silky mist.

Back in the busy city street, the police and an ambulance had been called, and while the police made measurements and calculations, the paramedics found for Troy, it was too late.

Push Your Luck

To take a risk on the assumption that you will continue to be successful even when continually risking all.

TO GET BACK HOME

Sir Edmund Brookton of Eiesen-Dasz Coreberg – a rich country which was located in the furthest reaches of the Continental European mainland – strode the flagstone walled corridors of the Palace of Whitehall, the largest palace in England and Europe with over fifteen hundred rooms. Many of the stone walls were covered in great colourful tapestries depicting religious scenes, which hung as decoration on the walls like large carpets. This year, 1599 saw Shakespeare's plays on at the Globe Theatre and Francis Drake and the other seagoing pirates and privateers of the time, bringing gold back to England from the New World (America).

Sir Edmund Brookton had arrived in England from his little-known country in the deepest part of the Continent to visit Her Majesty Queen Elizabeth, who was sometimes called The Virgin Queen (as she had never married), Gloriana or Good Queen Bess. As soon as he had arrived at court, Sir Edmund had sent gifts to the queen, consisting of fabulous diamonds and gold jewellery to introduce himself to her, and to hope that her courtiers would not search too long for the whereabouts of his home country. Of course, the Queen would not have heard of his homeland of Eiesen-Dasz Coreberg, because it didn't exist, and neither did Sir Edmund Brookton.

The man striding the stone floored corridors was in fact David Palmer of TEF, the Time Expeditionary Force, a new-found and highly secret government agency set up when time travel was first discovered, to search out major incidents and people of history. That the Force would have to be secret was extremely important, as anyone travelling in time and upsetting and changing history could of course cause catastrophic alterations to the future, and David Palmer had been highly trained to tread very carefully, indeed. Later, when other time travellers tried to alter historic events to create a better history for themselves, the Time Police was founded, to ensure history was not changed.

David, as the first time traveller for the Time Expeditionary Force, had been sent back from his future time era, and had materialised inside a small wooden-doored cupboard in Westminster Hall in London into the Tudor period.

The Elizabethan era was a time of sumptuary laws, which restricted what clothes a person could wear at court. This clothing restriction showed a person's status and wealth. For instance, a person with an income of twenty pounds per year was allowed to wear a satin doublet (a type of jacket) but not a satin gown, someone worth one hundred pounds per year could wear any satin but only velvet in a doublet. What these sumptuary laws did was to keep the lower orders of people in their place, as it was only the wealthy and powerful who could afford to wear quality clothes and pay the exorbitant prices for dyes to create differing colours.

Sir Edmund Brookton wore silk and satin in abundance, announcing him as super rich. He was tall, slim and handsome with long dark flowing hair, full beard and moustache, with dark eyes under black eyebrows, long thin nose and white teeth showing between a confident smile. He wore a ruff - a white collar which was around his neck and protruded all around for about ten centimetres - and also wore a richly purple coloured, long sleeved, pearl encrusted jacket above a doublet – a dark red covering from waist to thigh – and dark stockings and long black leather boots.

He entered the Great Hall, a massive room with a high ceiling twelve metres above and was also eight metres wide and at least sixty metres long. Its ceiling was made of oak roof beams which held up the tiled roof above and criss crossed the whole hall. The stone walls were covered in great multi coloured tapestries showing scenes of hunting and people picnicking in the forest. Hanging from the ceiling from long chains were chandeliers holding many candles, throwing flickering light around. On wooden tables, covered clay saucers held oil lamps which flickered a flame at its end. Because the windows of the great hall were high in the walls, so that not much sunlight reached inside, the flickering of the lamps and candles threw orange light everywhere. Also three enormous fire places lined the walls with roaring log-fuelled flames.

The great hall was crowded with people, standing around, talking and whispering. The men with their beards and moustaches, dressed in the thick white collar known as a ruff, with a dark shirt, tight jacket and cloak, and short puffed out pants and long stockings with flat shoes, and the ladies with brooches in their hair and also wearing the ruff collar; and colourful long sleeved dresses which puffed out at the hips and draped down to the ground.

Among the throng of people stood soldiers as royal guards, these men in their fashionable beards wore black brimmed round hats, a short ruff collar, a long sleeved red tunic showing the royal crest, and with puffed shoulders, a sword hanging from their belt, a short, red skirt and white stockings with black boots with red buckles.

Sir Edmund Brookton was greeted by one of the guards as soon as he entered the great hall, and recognised as a foreign visitor, then he was led to a throne-like seat in the middle of the hall. As they made their way through the throng of courtiers, the buzz of conversation stopped as the multitude of people stared in silence at the newcomer. The seat, when they arrived in the midst of the throng was gilded with gold and sparkled with swirling motifs and designs. In the seat sat Queen Elizabeth the First.

The Queen wore a tall sparkling tiara over her rather reddish hair, and her face was painted white with a make-up called ceruse - a mixture of white lead and vinegar - as was the fashion of the day, with her dark eyes and red painted lips showing brightly amid the strange whiteness. She also wore the fashionable ruff collar, and a long sleeved dress with studded diamonds attached and which had puffed shoulders and just below the waist the dress was hooped out around her hips, which reached down to her feet. The Queen's deep red cloak lay behind the throne-like chair.

The guard stood, half towards the queen and half towards David, as if expecting an assassination attempt from the visitor, then spoke in a loud voice for all the silenced crowd to hear. 'Your majesty, presenting Sir Edmund Brookton of Eiesen-Dasz Coreberg!' The guard stood back, a hand on the hilt of his sword as David stepped forward.

'Well, there you are Sir Edmund,' the Queen announced in a high voice, 'about time,' she said as she flashed a look at a diamond studded watch on her wrist. 'It is good to meet you, and thank you for the gifts you have sent me, I certainly cannot find fault with them. The gifts are very rich indeed, if I did complain you could quote of me: "The lady doth protest too much"'.

'Why, thank you, your majesty...' David stopped short in surprise, then leant forward, 'May I approach?'

'Of course,' the Queen answered and sent the guard away with a flourish of her hand, 'what is it Sir Edmund?'

'Ma'am,' he leaned forward and whispered, 'you've just looked at your wrist watch, and wrist watches weren't invented until the early twentieth century and you also just uttered the line "The lady doth protest too much" which was written into the play Hamlet, by William Shakespeare in the year 1600 and first performed on the stage in 1603. As this is the year 1599, you, like me, do not belong in this era, you must, therefore be a time traveller.'

'My lords!' the queen rose quickly from her seat as she spoke loudly, 'leave us! I must speak in private about political concerns with our distinguished Continental guest.' The surprised audience of courtiers, ladies and soldiers shuffled out of the great hall in silence, looking back in envy at the queen and her mysterious visitor.

'Well, you soon found me out,' the imposter queen said as soon as the great hall was empty of courtiers and guards, 'how did you know so quickly?'

'Because I studied Queen Elizabeth's life before I arrived here,' answered David, 'you obviously did not. I am the first time traveller, from the twenty-first century. Why are you here impersonating this queen, and where... I mean *when* are you from?'

'I am from the fiftieth century,' answered the imposter queen with a shy smile, 'my name's Jenna, and I came here because with all this white make up on my face I can just pass for the real queen, but mainly the fiftieth century is in a big mess. Governments around the globe are collapsing, law and order has broken down and warlords rule many lands. Manufacturing companies are closed down except for those making guns and munitions; politicians are assassinated every day as corruption rules the lands and pirates stopped sea travel many years ago, and aircraft can't fly without engines, fuel and mechanical parts being manufactured.

'If nuclear armaments were still usable - they were deemed too rusty and cobwebbed for further use – someone would have used them by now. There are no schools or hospitals since the breakdown and children and old people are sent out on a daily basis to forage for food and wood to burn for cooking and heating. The world is in a state of collapse. This Tudor world is more modern and more regulated than mine.

'We, the last scientists in England, maybe the last scientists in the world for all we know, found your twenty-first century mechanism for time travel in an old part of the barricaded building that we live in, and decided to go back to the only place the mechanism would take us, to your destination before us, the Tudor era, and there, we decided to marry Queen Elizabeth off to a Spanish king to create a new super power combining the very powerful sixteenth century Spain, France and Britain in the hope that as more and more countries, like America, are discovered and taken under its protective custody, a new world order would be made, keeping new territories within the new Royal family that we shall breed. This might sort out the terrible collapse of the far off future.'

'But anything could happen from this far back in time,' argued David, 'wars, royal families falling out, political upheaval, surely it would have been better to travel back to a later time, nearer your own era, to get help?'

'We had only one time travel option,' Jenna said, 'your one from the twenty-first century, and it led only here, to a cupboard in Westminster Hall.'

'And how do you get back to your century?' asked David, 'when you have done what you want here?'

'I don't get back,' Jenna said with a serious look, 'I will take the place of the queen, who is quite easy to impersonate, what with all the lead paint and make up. The real queen Elizabeth is on a hunting and visiting trip, and when she gets back tomorrow, I will discredit her as an imposter, marry a Spanish king or prince and lead the world onto a new history, in which Europe, Britain and later America will be part of a United Kingdom, kept together so that no one country becomes isolated, and no one nation wants to defeat another.'

'But surely it would be better to travel to a later, more nearer time to your own if you want to twist history into making a new future for you and your people?'

'Yes, I agree,' but we did not even know about your time travelling machinery,' answered Jenna, 'until we stumbled upon it in our archives, and its only destination was here, and there was not a method of getting back to the present; after using your system and travelling to the Tudor court, I must stay here and start a new dynasty.'

'Of course,' David said as he drew a small black box from his jacket and held it aloft, 'observe this. I step into the cupboard in Westminster Hall, press a button on this instrument, and I go instantly back to my time in the late twenty-first century. But it only has the ability to work once.'

'Why was it that the place to deliver you to this era was a cupboard in Westminster Hall?' Jenna asked

'If you send someone through time into the distant past,' explained David, 'that point that they arrive in may have been, hundreds, maybe thousands of years ago, a house, a barn, a factory, why, the traveller may have materialised inside a wooden beam or a tree or mangled inside a clockwork mechanism. Now Westminster Hall has stood since it was first built in the year 1099, it was refurbished in 1399 and still stands there now. So we knew that if we sent someone back in time to Westminster Hall, they would land somewhere safe. That's why we picked that cupboard. It has always been in that place, so if you travel anytime from 1099 it will always be there, you won't materialise inside a hill or something.

'And all of this has given me an idea. Take off the Elizabethan make up and come with me.'

Jenna scrubbed at her white painted face and tugged off the sparkling tiara from her head, pulled on the red cloak that lay at the foot of her seat and together they slipped quietly down the large corridors and left Whitehall Palace by a side door into the street known as Whitehall. Here David took off his flamboyant jacket and draped it, inside-out over his shoulder to try to mask its splendour, as a man of such seeming richness would not usually walk in the street among common people without a guard or entourage of servants.

The muddy street was alive with ragged street traders in their tall hats with long grey smocks with leather shoes for the men and head scarves and long sleeved drab dresses for the women. They offered for sale milk, cherries, shoes, trinkets and second hand clothes as they shuffled through the mud. Some people just sat and watched the world go by, with nothing to do. Wagons rolled along, drawn by oxen or horses, and grander folk rode by on horseback or in closed wooden carriages with attendant coach driver and footmen.

Jenna and David walked under the arch of the giant Holbein Gate, the three storied building which stood in the middle of the road as they passed the large houses on either side of the muddy street, and so on to New Palace Yard in which stood Westminster Hall; nearby stood an old clock tower which had no round face near the top with hands to show the time, but which rang bells to mark the passing hours. As they approached the Hall, David put back on his jacket to show his obvious richness of dress, which would stop anyone questioning them as they approached the building.

The magnificent hammer-beam roof of Westminster Hall is the largest medieval timber roof in Northern Europe. Measuring twenty one by seventy three metres long, it has been a centre of administration and a law court for hundreds of years.

David and Jenna slipped in among the many people already in the Hall; lawyers in high stiff collars and flowing robes, and messengers in dark jackets and loose trousers and stockings, all striding busily by, servants in liveried uniforms carrying loaded up trays, and priests in black robes and engrossed clerics in dark clothes with cloaks hurrying along on many government jobs, all wearing the fashionable ruff collar.

The two walked down past the granite slabs of the massive walls and into a smaller corridor until they stood in front of the wooden door of the cupboard where they had both appeared from their own times.

'Here we are,' announced David, opening the door to show Jenna its empty interior, 'I have the device to return to my time. It will only work once... Oh! Someone's coming!'

'I can't hear anyone...' Jenna said in surprise, looking both ways down the corridor.

'Quick. Get inside the cupboard.' David ordered. As Jenna stepped inside the cupboard, David jammed the door closed behind her, and took from his pocket the small oblong device. 'Jenna,' he said to her through the closed door, 'you were right, there wasn't anybody coming along, I'm afraid I tricked you into entering the cupboard. This device I can only use once. Once I press its activating button, you will be transferred to my time, where I'm sure the people of my era can help you to organise your future better than you altering history by replacing this Tudor queen right now. Explain to my people in the twenty-first century about the breakdown in the future and I'm sure they will help you. To create a new very large twist in history at this very early time could go terribly wrong. So I'm sending you back to my time...'

'But what about you,' came Jenna's muffled voice from behind the oak door, 'what will become of you?'

'Well, I know I can't get back,' David sighed, 'but I think it's the best thing for the future of the world's history. I'll take back the gifts I sent to you as a queen, then I'll have plenty of money to set myself up with a good house and a business, after all I know what the future will need, so I'll invent a new business. I should have a good living. I will settle down here in this time. Goodbye.' David pressed the button on the little device and sent Jenna away off into the future.

The next day, to all the court's surprise, Queen Elizabeth returned from her hunting trip.

Clutch at Straws

Try any route to get out of a desperate situation, no matter how unlikely it is to succeed.

The magnificent hammer beam roof
of Westminster Hall

DON'T BE TOO SURE

The rusty old white Transit van with two wooden ladders roped to its roof rack buzzed along in the busy high street traffic. Printed in four lines on the van's side were the legends:

B. TRAINER
GENERAL BUILDER
FREE ESTIMATES
ALL WORK GUARANTEED

followed by a contact telephone number for a mobile phone. The van suddenly swung to the left and turned down into a side road. After a while the Transit wheezed to a jerky stop outside number eleven Mayford Avenue, a quiet tree-lined street off the main road. It was a tidy road filled with older style houses with trim, mowed lawns, asphalt driveways and tiny garages on the side, too small for a modern car. Most of the windows of the houses in Mayford Avenue were double glazed with white frames and had lace curtains behind them, and had brightly painted front doors.

Bert Trainer, the plump driver of the battered Transit, rubbed his stubbly chin as he looked at number eleven, 'I'll be in the transport cafe by lunch time today,' he muttered to himself, 'with a tasty few twenty pound notes in me pocket.' He'd noticed number eleven before, as he had driven through this street; there were a few houses here that appeared to be very quiet and he'd noted that the occupants of the quiet ones seemed usually to be single ladies, some old dears living on their own. Bert grinned to himself, he was sixty five years old but just couldn't even think of retirement; life was too good at the moment, business was booming.

Bert had lots of greying brown hair sticking out of the sides of his old blue baseball cap which covered the top of his bald head, long-haired fluffy dark eyebrows, dark brown eyes and a large nose stuck in a weathered reddish cheeked face with brown teeth. Bert's famous "plumber's cleavage" showed itself as he scrambled backwards from the van; as his worn old hipster denims slid low and his faded blue T-shirt rode up. He straightened up by the side of the van on his battered black trainers, pulled his shirt down over his large belly, hoisted up his denims over his bum, locked the door of the van and strode for the pavement, as he stuck the van's ignition keys into his back pocket.

Once on the pavement, Bert stepped up to, and pushed open the garden gate of number eleven, and looking up, made tut, tut noises as he marched up the small strip of tarmac to the house and rapped hard with his knuckles on the glass window of the front door. 'Whoever's that?' came a faint female voice from the other side of the door, somewhere in the house. Bert continued to tut as he rapped even more. The door was opened by Ellen Hartson, a thin eighty five year old lady with permed blonde hair, soft make up and pale lipstick, in a dark silky top with a silver star pattern, black trousers and low heeled shoes. 'Whatever's wrong?' Ellen asked, 'why are you rapping on my front door's window?'

'Is the man of the house in?' Bert demanded with a snort in a pushy way.

'Man of the house?...' Ellen faltered, 'why, why no, my husband passed away...'

'Gable's gawn.' Bert began to tut again as he looked up at the outside of the house.

'I beg your pardon?' Ellen asked, puzzled, 'gablesgawn? What does that mean?'

'Look,' Bert said stepping back and pointing upwards, to the gable roof over the upstairs bedroom, 'gable's gawn. It's leaning outward. And that's gonna cost you five hundred smackers.' Ellen followed Bert out and stared up at the bedroom's gabled roof.

'There's nothing wrong with that,' Ellen said, 'it's not really leaning at all,' as Bert walked passed her and through the front door into the hall. 'And, by the way,' she continued, 'I don't remember inviting you in to my house.'

'Yeah, it *is* leaning out,' said Bert with an authoritative snort, 'I'm a master builder, I should know. And the guttering will be twisted as well, that'll be another three hundred quid. An' when I repair the gable, it'll move most of the roof tiles, so they'll have to be checked and replaced. I s'pose I *could* take a look at the rest of the house for you, while I'm at it. You're lucky I happened to pass by this way. I'm Bert Trainer, call me Bert.' Bert sat on the sofa in the living room as Ellen closed the front door with a deep sigh. He looked around the cozy living room with its colourful deep carpet, large TV, soft drape curtains, lamp holders and shiny wooden coffee table. Ellen returned to her living room and sat on an armchair opposite Bert. 'No chance of a cuppa, I s'pose?' Bert asked.

'Of course,' I'll make one presently,' smiled Ellen, 'so you're a builder Mister, Bert. Do you come with recommendations?'

'What? What d'yer mean, recommendations, like?' Bert asked with a frown.

'Recommendations, you know, recommendations,' Ellen smiled, 'it's when you've done a good building job for someone or other and they would recommend your work and yourself to other people, and they say you always do a good job, and are reliable and not too expensive. You know, recommendations.'

'Oh,' said Bert with a frown, 'recommendations... Well I did a job for Mrs err... Mrs err... Collingwood last week, she was happy with my work.'

'And she would recommend you to me, would she?' Ellen asked.

'Oohh! Yes, of course she would,' Bert smiled a grim smile from the corner of his mouth.

'Could you give me Mrs Collingwood's address,' asked Ellen, 'or her phone number, so's I can call her?'

'Yeah, her phone number,' answered Bert, 'I'll get it for you in a minute. Or maybe her address.'

'That's good,' said Ellen as she leaned behind her seat and picked up a mobile telephone, 'I've just got to make a quick call.' Bert continued to look around the room from his seat on the sofa, occasionally shaking his head and tut, tutting as he realised another job that he could charge for.

Ellen tapped in numbers on her mobile and waited patiently as she and Bert heard the ring tone. 'Hello...' came a muffled reply, as the phone call was answered.

'Hello, is that the police station?' Ellen said. Bert suddenly went strangely quiet.

'Yes,' came the muffled reply from the phone, 'Moresome Green Police Station, what can we do for you?'

Ellen continued to talk in her soft and friendly way, 'could I speak to Sergeant George Hartson, please?.. Yes, I know he's the senior uniformed officer... Yes, I know he's busy... No, it's not an emergency... Well, I'm sure he will talk to me if you tell him it's his mum calling?'

There was a loud click from the speaker of Ellen's mobile phone. 'Oh, Hello, George darling,' Ellen said into the phone's microphone, 'it's mum. I've got a mister Bert Trainer here. He wants to do some work on the house... Yes, yes, of course I've got the CCTV camera working on the outside of the house recording all the number plates in the street... You will... Oh that is good of you... I'm sure mister Trainer will explain to you or your colleagues exactly what work he wants to do... A gablesgawn, yes, gawn, I'm not sure what that means, exactly, it must be a technical term, but I'm sure that was what it was he said... Alright then dear, I'll see you soon.' Ellen clicked off her mobile telephone.

'Err, I've err, got to get something from the van,' Bert suddenly blustered and stood up as if he had been stung, 'I'll get you Mrs err... Mrs err... Collins' address or phone number, it's in the glove box in the van.' He marched quickly from the living room into the hall where he opened the front door, stepped out and banged the door closed behind him. Ellen stood up and walked over to her living room windows and watched Bert from between the Venetian blinds.

Bert walked quickly to his trusty, rusty van, fumbling with

the keys as he went. As soon as he arrived at the van he unlocked the door with a shaky hand, as he looked left and right with a panicky look on his face. Then he jumped in, started the vehicle which made a tired roar, then crunched the gears, and finally, with a squeal of tyre rubber, drove off leaving a cloud of diesel fumes hanging in the street like a blue cloud behind him.

Ellen smiled to herself; the builder Bert thought that he could take all her money doing jobs around her home which didn't really need doing, well he'd had another think coming. She turned back in her living room and once again took out her mobile phone. She dialled the same numbers she had dialled when Bert had been in the room. 'Hello...' came a muffled reply.

'Oh, hello Maisy,' Ellen said into the phone,' it's me again: Ellen. Our idea worked. Thanks for remembering our scheme to answer as though it is the police when I say "Hello, is that the police station?" That man Bert thought I was talking to a son of mine and soon disappeared when he thought a policeman was on the way. So, thank you. I'll do the same for you, anytime. Just say: "Hello, is that the police station?"'

'Oh, good, great. Well done.' came the reply from Maisy, 'perhaps now us older folk can be left in peace.'

Don't count.......

Don't count your chickens before they are hatched. Don't be hasty in evaluating one's assets. To have "Another Think Coming" is to be so sure of yourself as to think that you can do as you wish, only to be shown otherwise.

WHERE THE BUCK STOPS

At the end of a country lane in leafy Dene's Forest with its acres of grassy meadows, tall trees and green bushes, stood the white three storey building with the words painted down its side: **IONIC INDUSTRIES (UK)**. In its grey tarmac surfaced car park below the building, Matthew Connelly slumped himself down with a thump into the driver's seat of the battered old red Mini car and pulled the door closed with a jerk. He inserted the key into the ignition, closed his eyes and said a small prayer to himself in silence. Then he turned the key and – whump! the engine started, first time! 'Great,' he thought, 'I'll give it a minute for the engine to warm up, as its started without any trouble for once.' He turned his eyes to the interior mirror and looked at himself.

He looked tired. He had short dark hair, shaved at the sides of his head, thin eyebrows over brown eyes, which looked slightly red-rimmed, a short nose and straight mouth with fairly even teeth, and he had a thin, whispy moustache and beard that looked as if it would blow away in a strong breeze. He wore his usual long-sleeved white shirt and tight fitting long grey trousers and brown leather shoes. Matthew sighed as he looked at his reflection in the drivers' mirror.

Twenty eight years old and he looked tired after a day at the office. And it wasn't as if it was a hard day's toil at the office, after all, he worked at a research facility, looking for new ways to use sub-atomics in industry.

His research was his job, and also his deep interest, but his real love was electron clouds. Most people see the usual graphic of an atom and see the nucleus in the middle and the electrons flying around like tiny planets around a sun, but it isn't really like that, electrons don't fly round in nice circles, they spin round together in clouds. Matthew could see that there was a long term future for using electron clouds, in industry and of course, national defence. But at the age of twenty eight, he would have to wait until he was a fair bit older, with years of experience in the nucleonics field before he would be listened to, by the bosses of Ionic Industries (UK) about his ideas for the nuclear-powered future.

Matthew knew that he was well thought of at Ionic, but only time would tell if it was his long-term future, and for now he had to spend time working every day to prove himself. He was not that well paid either, that would come with experience and achievement, as only the successful boys in research institutes get the big bucks, so for now, he was a young man with a wife and two little daughters to think about.

He put the humming Mini car into gear, raised the revs a bit, lifted the clutch gently as he released the handbrake and ouhh! - the engine stalled. 'Oh no!' Matthew cried, 'not again! It's conked out!' He twisted the key; the starter motor whirled and turned the engine, but no, it would not start. Matthew sat for a moment in frustrated silence. This car was so important to him and his family. The research company of Ionic Industries was a great place to be employed, but it was stuck out in the middle of the countryside in Dene's Forest, meaning that you had to have transport just to get to work. In this car he ferried his daughters Chloe, six, and eight year old Lisa to school in the morning, then on to the supermarket where his wife Francis worked, then finally on to Ionic. At five in the afternoon, when Matthew finished his working day, he would drive to his mum's, where the girls would be, after being picked up from school by his mum, and where Francis would go after work and the three members of his family would wait for him to arrive and take them home in the car. And now the car once again had let him down.

Around him cars were being started up and driven off, as the car park slowly emptied of his fellow workers and researchers. He sat and waited, and waited, to give the battery time to accumulate, or something, as he had been told to do. Then he suddenly turned the ignition key. Woww... woww... the electric starter motor screeched like a chased cat. Then went silent.

Matthew sighed and reached for his mobile phone. As soon as Francis' phone began to ring, his wife answered: 'Hi Matt, car let you down again?' In his mind's eye, Matthew could see his wife's face, with her long dark hair, smooth tanned face with open friendly smile.

'Yeah, it's so annoying,' Matthew said, 'we've got to ditch this motor...'

'We can't afford it, Matt,' Francis stated flatly, 'look, I'll go to your mum's, pick up the girl's and take them home on the bus, don't worry. But get yourself out of the car park before they close the gates, even if you have to push the car out. You won't be able to get it going if it's locked up in the car park for the night by the security guards.'

'Yes, of course,' Matthew knew he had to get moving, 'I'll see you at home, then. Bye Francis.' Matthew noted that the car park was indeed quickly emptying, with employees driving off all the time, there were now only the posh motors of the top boys left. There was a blue Bentley, owned by the boss of Ionic, Mr T. W. Hamilton – who Matthew had never met - then there were two black Jaguars, owned by the two Research Team Leaders, and a very low-built gold and blue two seater super sports car, probably a high flying visitor to the research and development company.

'Right,' Matthew said to himself, 'one last go.' He twisted the ignition key and – whump! the engine started immediately. Matthew selected first gear, and raised the revs high; he had to get out of the gates before the car park was empty, or he'd have to leave the car there and walk down the country lane until he came to the main road and the bus stop. At least if he got outside into the lane, he could work on the engine until late, in the hope of keeping it running.

As soon as the Mini was on the move he kept his foot on the gas; he wasn't gong to chance changing gear in case it stalled again. Then he was out of the gate. At last! 'Hey,' he thought, 'I might as well see how far I can go.' He stayed on the lane and chanced selecting second gear. 'Every metre is a metre nearer home,' he smiled to himself. It was getting just a bit dark, so he switched on the car's sidelights, but he wasn't going to put on the car's headlights until he got to the main road, he didn't want to deprive the battery of any energy. He motored steadily on down the lane.

Suddenly the whole lane lit up with a blinding white light. The green leaves of the trees and grass verges where highlighted, as was the silvery tarmac of the lane. Matthew squinted at his interior mirror at the searchlight dazzling him from behind. It was the gold and blue sports car from the Ionic car park. The hyper sports car zoomed up behind him as he squeezed himself near to the grass verge on the left of the lane. The driver of the car flashed the powerful lights at the back of the Mini and flew by in a roar of noise and rushing wind.

The lane went dark again as Matthew switched on his headlights onto dipped beam. The car that had overtaken him sprinted to a bend in the lane and turned. Then – a booming crashing sound followed by a great flash! A flame shot into the air from around the corner! Then a cloud of black smoke rose, billowing upward. Matthew floored the accelerator and arrived at the bend in the lane. The super car was on its side – and it was alight!

The sports car had left the lane and shot over the verge where it had hit a tree head on. The tree had smashed in the front of the vehicle and turned the car over on its side and now flames were rising from its buckled front end. The tree trunk that the car had hit was still rocking back and forth, leaves and branches falling onto the flames of the car, adding to the smoke and blaze.

Matthew drove the Mini onto the lane's verge, braked hard and shuddered to a halt on the grass behind the sports car. He stared open-mouthed at the scene before him, frozen in motion as he watched. Then reality snapped in. He jumped up, switching off the engine – 'Oh no!' he cried out loud, 'I shouldn't have switched off!' He once again turned the ignition key – nothing, the engine was dead. And he was stopped very close to the rear bumper of the stricken super car.

Still he sat for more seconds in indecision: this was one of those important *Where the Buck Stops* moments. He had to make a decision. There was no-one else around; either he did something, or nothing would happen. He alone had to act. Then he spoke out loud: 'I've got to help!' Matthew jumped out of the stalled Mini and ran to the car in front. Now he was at the car he could hear the hiss of escaping steam, and feel the heat of the flames from the front of the vehicle. Although the flames were only about thirty centimetres high – they were getting bigger! He tried to open the driver's door which was facing upwards as the car was on its left side. The door was too heavy for him to lean over and lift.

Matthew jumped onto the side of the car, bent down and pulled hard at the door handle. This time the door opened upwards and Matthew saw the driver, a dark skinned man with black hair, moustache and beard, wearing a white shirt, dark tie and an expensive dark blue suit. He had a very bad gash on his forehead and his nose and lip was bleeding, he was sitting in his seat trying to release his seat belt; he looked dazed and disorientated as he fumbled his hands along the belt. 'Come on, mate,' Matthew urged as he leaned in and undid the seat belt clip. Then as the man began to sink lower into the side-on car, he reached in and grabbed the man under the arm and round his neck.

'Oohh!' Matthew grunted as he dragged the driver out onto the right hand side of the car which was facing upwards. He slid the man down to the ground by the side of the vehicle.

'We must save the Kalifa,' mumbled the dark man, as he staggered by the car, his eyes glazed, 'he is my employer and my friend.' Matthew looked down into the passenger compartment of the car and there slumped down by the passenger door which was pressing onto the ground, was another man, very similar to the man Matthew had pulled from the burning motor; dark hair, full beard, dark suit. He was unconscious and he too had a large gash on his forehead.

Matthew gently but quickly dropped down into the driver's seat and undid the knocked-out man's seat belt. 'Listen, mate,' he said as quickly as he could, 'this car is alight and might go up in a big bang any minute. I know that if you have internal injuries and I yank you up through the open doorway above us, I may injure you further. But if I don't pull you out and this lot goes up in smoke we may go with it unless we act now.'

Matthew grabbed the man by the shirt collar and stood up on the central gear selector, resting the heavy weight of the man on the side of the passenger seat. He then clambered out of the car and knelt on the side of the bodywork, then leaned in and grabbed him again.

As the flames grew higher from the front of the car, Matthew gave one almighty heave with all his strength; he lifted the man out of the car and he fell, with Matthew onto the grass nearby. 'Come on!' Matthew shouted as he grabbed the fallen one and began to drag him away from the stricken car, followed by the half conscious driver who he had got out of the car earlier.

He dragged the man from the super sports car and got behind his Mini, bringing the dazed passenger with them. 'Keep behind my car. I think she's going to go...' Boom! The sports car exploded into a massive ball of flame, throwing metal bits and burning parts around. Within a few moments the car was a roaring fire, but Matthew and the two men were safe behind the Mini.

Breathlessly, Matthew dialled 999 on his mobile phone and soon an Ambulance and the Fire Brigade were on their way.

As soon as they arrived, the firefighters jumped from their vehicles and were combating the blazing car with sprays and foam-dousing hoses, clattering round and keeping onlookers, which seemed to come out of the trees, away from the blaze. At the same time, the ambulance men, who had arrived with the firefighters, tended to the two men from the car, who were still lying in the safety of the protection of the stranded Mini.

Sometime later, after being checked out himself by the paramedics, and then telling the police the full story of the accident and the ensuing blazing car, Matthew saw that the front of his Mini had been spattered with burning debris and was itself burned, buckled and disfigured. Even later still, he was dropped home in a police car to tell his wife and girls that the Mini would no longer be a problem for them as they no longer had a car.

The next day Matthew arrived at work on an old bicycle that he had borrowed from a neighbour. The talk all through Ionic research and development was about the car crash of the visitors to the company. Though both passengers had been injured, neither was seriously hurt. Matthew was pleased about that and wondered what would happen about his transport and if the insurance would cover the cost of the repair or replacement of his vehicle.

A week went by, a week of pedalling to work on the old bike and taking the girls early to school by bus and another bus to the supermarket for Francis' job. Then out of the blue, an internal email informed him that he was to report to the top level of the Ionic building, to the office of none other than the big boss himself, Mr T. W. Hamilton.

Matthew glanced into the mirror of the staff toilet before leaving his place in the research department and wished he was wearing a suit and tie instead of his usual long sleeved shirt and grey trousers, but there was nothing he could do about it now. And what did the boss want with him, anyway? Promotion? Of course! He saw himself, in his mind's eye, accepting a pay rise and being given his own office by the boss. But in reality, that was extremely, remotely, unlikely. And anyway, he realised, he hadn't actually been up close to the boss, ever before, and had only seen the man from a distance, a tall man with wild hair and thick glasses. How would Matthew greet him? What would he say?

He pressed the button for the elevator, stepped into its plush steel and glass interior and watched the red indicator buttons rise with the movement as he rose through the two floor levels. The elevator stopped with a bump. The doors swished open. 'Ah! Mister Matthew Connelly, I presume?' A man stepped forward with his right hand outstretched.

Matthew blinked and felt his throat go dry, as T. W. Hamilton gripped and shook. his hand. Matthew saw the wild straggly hair, that he had seen from a distance, now towering over him. The straggly brownish hair hung in twisty bits but his hair was actually quite thin, he noted now that he was close up. He wore spectacles with brown frames over his intense greyish eyes, squat nose and big smiling mouth. He had on a tan coloured shirt with a tie that was hanging from one side of the collar, and a crumpled brown suit with blue trainers on his feet. 'Yes... yes,' Matthew choked as he spoke, 'I'm Matthew Connelly, pleased to meet you Mister Hamilton.'

T. W. Hamilton led Matthew into his office with its large windows looking out onto the car park below, and the forest beyond. A big oak desk sat in the middle of the office with a computer screen sitting on it, and a large wooden, leather padded swivel seat behind. Some cupboards lined along the walls and there was a cluster of chairs in front of the desk. Sitting in two of the chairs were two men. Both were dark skinned with black hair, moustache and beard, wearing white shirts, dark blue ties and expensive dark blue suits. Both had a bandaged foreheads. 'Oh, it's you,' Matthew faltered, 'the guys from the burning car.'

'Yes, it is us,' said the man on the left,' as he stood up, 'I am Saba Hasan, member of the Royal Household and this gentleman is His Royal Highness Kalifa bin al Said. We are from the United Arab World.'

'Indeed, we are,' spoke the second man rising from his seat and walking over to Matthew, 'and we owe you our lives. You saved us from the burning wreck of that car.'

'Oh, well...' Matthew flustered, 'it's OK... I mean, it was nothing... Err, my pleasure...'

'I understand,' continued HRH Kalifa bin al Said, 'that our car ruined your own vehicle, a Mini I believe? I would like to replace it for you.'

'Oh well, it was just an old Mini...' spluttered Matthew,

'and the insurance...'

'No, no,' continued HRH the Kalifa, 'please forget your old car and accept a small gift from those who you saved. There is a Mini car dealership in the nearby town. I have ordered you a top of the range new Mini, and would be ever grateful if you would accept it from me. It is waiting for you to go and pick it up.'

'Well, that's fantastic,' Matthew couldn't stop grinning, 'thank you so much.' Matthew backed from the trio of men towards the elevator, feeling grateful but also out of place.

'Oh, and Matthew,' T. W. Hamilton said as Matthew pressed the button for the lift, 'we, that's the two gentlemen here, and our other research people have been looking into the future of electron clouds, in sub atomics, and I see that it is your subject. Well, that's just what we need. I'm upgrading you to our higher research department, if you would like to join us?'

'Why, it's just what I've wanted,' Matthew answered with unmistakable glee.

'Of course it comes into a higher pay bracket,' smiled T. W. Hamilton, 'but for now, let me get one of our chaps to run you down into town to pick your new Mini.'

The Buck Stops Here

Responsibility is not passed on beyond this point.

Have you read Terry's Time Police Trilogy ?

The Police travelling through time to stop the arch criminal Draco changing history so as to control the world. The stories tell of their struggles to maintain history as we know it, in their quest they cover many periods of history, from the Ice Age, to the Princes in Tower to World War ll

The Time Police

The Time Police 2
- *Draco Returns*

The Time Police 3
- *Invasion*

TUNNEL VISION

The very large area of green countryside, boarded around on all sides as a building site, was quiet. The diggers and drillers were silent, but a few safety helmeted workers with their yellow hi-viz jackets and over-trousers were still present, pottering around the new construction site. The silent foundation diggings were situated in Farnesleigh de-la-Zouch, a once small village, twenty kilometres outside the city, which had been abandoned in the seventeenth century, and now only a deserted hillside remained.

A gate opened in the building site boarded-up area, and a black saloon car was driven in after being checked by two uniformed security officers who had been standing guard at the gates to the site. The car drove through the grass and mud up to one of the two single-storey mobile offices which had been placed on the site for the managers of the construction. Two casually-dressed men got out of the car and climbed the wooden stairs to the yellow and grey pre-fabricated building; the door opened from inside for them as they got to the top of the small steps, and they entered.

The interior of the office was typical: there were small windows on both sides of the room looking out onto the construction area and large maps and lists, agendas, rotas and safety laws hung from the walls. A large brown desk stood in the middle of the room with six chairs facing it and a swivel chair behind it, and sitting in the swivel chair at the desk sat a large, silver haired man wearing a grey shirt, white tie and a light grey suit, who was talking quietly into a telephone. The two visitors were ushered to the chairs in front of the desk, where they sat.

The man who had shown the two visitors to their seats walked a few paces on and stood against the opposite wall, behind the man at the desk. He was Mark Long, an experienced building worker and tunneller, who wore the usual yellow safety helmet and hi-viz outer coat and over-trousers with steel-tipped boots. He had the ruddy complexion of a man who does not work inside but is used to the open air, with brown eyes, strong nose and a set mouth on a stubbly chin. 'Hi, gents,' he said in a strong voice, 'I'm Mark Long, construction engineer, and I'm in charge of digging the foundations on this plot. The gentleman here in the chair, is Mr Owen Wallis, managing director of Owen Construction, who are building a transmission substation here. Now, I don't know if you are familiar with electricity step-down substations, but to explain: it is an area where power lines meet, and which decreases the voltage of incoming electric power, allowing it to connect from long distance high voltage transmission, to local lower voltage distribution. It also re-routes power to other transmission lines that serve local markets, which will power the new town which is planned to be built near to this area.'

Mister Owen Wallis, who had been telephoning from his seat now put down his telephone and looked up smiling at the two visitors. He was a bulkily built man with silvery white hair and eyebrows over dark eyes. His face seemed lined with the concerns of a large company, with a sharp nose and clean shaven chin. 'Gentlemen,' he announced in a weary voice, 'thank you for coming to see us today, at such short notice. You are the experts I have requested to come here? You're from the local archaeological society, I believe?'

'Yes, we are,' said the man in the left seat, 'I am Andrew Walker, President of the Farnesleigh and District Archaeological Society, and this is our librarian, Bernard Hughes. Why have you called us here mister Wallis? What can we do for you?' Owen Wallis looked carefully at Andrew Walker and saw an older man with white straggly hair, blue-grey eyes, thin nose and pursed lips. He wore an old brown suit over a white shirt and brown tie with dusty black shoes.

Then Owen Wallis glanced at Bernard Hughes the archaeological societies librarian, a tall, thin, brown eyed, bald man with a fixed expression of concern on his face, with a bony nose upon which were perched rimless reading glasses, which he peered over. He wore a checked shirt beneath an old blue cardigan, brown corduroy trousers and brown soft shoes.

Owen Wallis sat back in his swivel chair, took in a deep breath and began: 'We, and by that I mean *my* company, were given the contract to build the transmission substation here, on this site. I point out here, on this site because I didn't know, until we started digging the foundations that beneath the grass on this land there used to be a church here, nor was I aware of its history...'

'Well, we of course know the story of the church of Saint Michael, Farnesleigh de-la-Zouch,' said Andrew Walker, 'it was founded here in the twelfth century, serving the very small community of the village. And it has not been used or visited for hundreds of years.'

'And the village was abandoned?' asked Owen Wallis, 'why was that?'

'I can tell you the village's history,' Bernard Hughes spoke for the first time, 'it was founded in the twelfth century, but it was not a real success, it's ground was fairly poor and making a living as a farmer was difficult, but people soldiered on, scraping a life out of the land. During the Black Death - the bubonic plague of the fourteenth century - it was nearly completely deserted, as most of the villagers died of the plague. But somehow, a dribble of survivors stayed. Then after hundreds of poor years, along came the factories in the seventeen eighties, at the start of the industrial revolution.

'Now, the factories employed a great number of people for labour, men, women and children, but the factories needed power, and steam power had not been invented in the early days of the start of the machine industry. So the factories were constructed near rivers, where the river water could be guided over water wheels to drive the mechanicals inside the factory.

'So, when a factory was opened by the nearby river Wandell, the few people left in Farnesleigh deserted the village and moved to housing supplied by the factory, to get employment. They abandoned the village completely.'

'And that's the end of the village's story?' asked Owen.

'Well, there's not a lot to tell,' answered Andrew, 'over the many years which followed, wooden beams, roof tiles, stone blocks and anything that could be used for construction was taken from the abandoned village and church, which slowly sank into the hillside. There was a small graveyard attached to the church, but I think it's location is not now known. Is this why you have called us here? To ask about an old, forgotten church?'

'I think Mark should continue our story at this point,' announced Owen, 'let him tell you what happened to him.'

'OK,' Mark Long stepped up to the desk and stood by his employer, 'two days ago I began the first part of my job here; we started to dig down for the deep foundations of the substation. All began well, until one of the digger drivers called me to report that he had dug through into a large empty space. I took a quick look and then gathered a couple of experienced guys around me, and we got lots of gear together and a ladder and we descended into the hole in the ground.

'As soon as I landed on the floor of the large underground space, and we had lit up our torches and helmet lights, I knew it had been a church. Although the floor was slightly angled, it was strong and made of flagstones. The walls were blocks of rough stone and in the beams of our lights, we could see small crucifixes and statues, covered in thick dust, that had been left there on the floor, over many, many years.

'The stone stairway that had once led to the main church upstairs was filled with stones, and large boulders and earth blocked the way, but further on, at the end of the crypt, was a small tunnel entrance. We entered the tunnel, which went on for a fair few metres then we came to a point where two tunnels led off from the one we were in; one to the left and one to the right. We took the right tunnel for no reason, but then, after passing through a twisting tunnel, we came to another two tunnels, one to the left and one to the right. This time we retraced our steps until we were back in the crypt of the old church.

'Well now, we had tracking devices, sat-nav, a compass

and GPS, but mainly we relied on a very large ball of string, which we attached to a stone statue in the crypt and explored the tunnel system, knowing that we couldn't get lost; we could always follow the trail of the string back to the crypt.

'Well, we followed all the tunnels beneath the ground leading from the crypt of the church. All the tunnels ended with a stone wall, a place where for some reason the excavators of the tunnel system had just stopped digging. Except for one. This tunnel, the longest of them all, this one that led furthest from the church, twisting this way and that with many more tunnels leading off, this one also suddenly stopped. But this time it did not end in a place where digging had just stopped; it was a wall of sheer stone, it looked as if the land at the end of the tunnel had just slid down in front of the cavern, it was a solid rock end.'

'So, that was it?' Andrew asked, eyebrows raised, 'that was the end of it?'

'No artefacts?' Bernard questioned, 'nothing to indicate what had been in the tunnels?'

'Yes, and it's the reason we called you,' Mark said, 'if the villagers abandoned the place in the seventeen eighties, and the secret tunnels were already under the ground beneath the church, at that date, how long has this been down there?' He drew something from beneath Owen's desk and put it on the desk top.

Andrew and Bernard leaned forward to see; it was a bag of some sort, made out of a loose knitted sacking material. Bernard put out a hand to take it... 'Stop! It's disintegrating with every touch,' Mark explained. 'Let me show you its contents.' He carefully opened the stiff and crackly bag and withdrew some faded paperwork. As he spread it out on the desk before him, the paper cracked and some small pieces flaked off the edges. 'It's a letter of some sort, made up of some pages,' Mark continued, looking at the words on the crackly page, 'but I can't really begin to understand what it says, it's in a foreign language. I can make out some of the words, it says "As thai haf writen half I al in my inglish sai", I don't really understand a word.'

'Why, that's early English, when the language changed from the Norman French into English,' Bernard said with surprise, 'I've studied it for years.'

'Could you read this?' Owen asked eagerly, 'can we find out what it says and when it is from?'

'Let me try,' Bernard shuffled his chair up to the desk where Mark carefully twisted the papers around for him to see. Bernard pushed his glasses back onto the higher part of his nose and began to read aloud:

'It is the year of our Lord 1348, the year of the plague known as the black death.

We are three: I am Hugo, church sexton at Saint Michael's church, I have lived here in the village all of my twenty five years of life, where our friar, who died of the plague yesterday taught me to read and write. Then there is Odo, a local man who is older than me. And Milus, a young man from the fields.

Four weeks ago a relative of one of the villagers died of the plague in London and his neighbours sent the dead man's old clothes to him. Within days of the old clothes arriving, the plague began, large swellings grew on people's arms, legs and necks, the swellings turned black, they bled, and the blood was black mixed with green scum. Then the people were sick with fever, vomited and were delirious, and died within a day. The village was almost empty of people in a matter of a week. We, us three, were hiding in the crypt of the church, too afraid to go out, as the plague was killing everybody. Our families were all dead.

We were starving, and without water, cowering in the crypt of the church too afraid to go out in case we met one of the few remaining villager's who would infect us. Our only clothes are what we always stand in; smock, loose trousers and soft leather shoes. That was when Milus found the entrance to the tunnel at the end of the crypt.

With sparks from my tinder box we lit one of the two tapers that we had found in the crypt and followed the tunnel, the light flickering upon the grey carved walls. Often we could come to a fork, where we chose which way to go, we just guessed which way, all we wanted was to get out of Farnesleigh. The tunnels seemed to go on forever and ever, our tapers burned out, and Milus began a non-stop mumbling of prayers. Then turning a corner, our way was barred by roots and green leaves from a large plant. We pushed the greenery to one side and passed through.

We were outside. It was night. Before us was a sight that stopped us in our tracks: we stood transfixed, mouths open. Across the green of the grass where we stood was a city, I knew it was a city although I had never seen a city before, it just had to be. It stretched for as far as the eye could see in all directions and every house, church and building in the city shone with a bright white light and together all the lights lit up the night sky. Milus began to cry.

'We must go to the city,' I said, 'to see if we can get help for Farnesleigh while it is in the midst of a plague epidemic.'

'We cannot,' Odo cried in fear, 'for it will be the devil's home.'

'The Lord will not be able to save us,' groaned Milus tearfully, 'we must go and never come back.' I pleaded with them and after some arguments, we walked on. Soon we came to a river which shimmered with silver light reflected from the city, where hundreds of ships careened by at fantastic speeds.

Imagine our shock and surprise when we approached the river to find that it was not a river but a ribbon of solid material which reflected the light, and the ships upon it were wheeled vehicles without any animals to pull them along, but screamed and screeched, howled and thundered as they sped past us at tremendous velocities, each with powerful lights which blinded us. Poor Milus could take it no more; he fell to his knees in frightful prayer, then fled away, not back towards the tunnels whence we had come, but along the side of the shiny roadway, shouting for the Lord to save us. We never saw him again.

We sat down at the side of this roaring horror as the vehicles raced past, not knowing how to get to the city. As time went by, the amount of the hurtling monsters screaming their way by us, grew less, and Odo and I waited until a large gap between the speeding leviathans appeared. 'Come, Hugo,' cried Odo with a panic in his voice, 'now is the only chance to get to the city beyond.' We ran.

On the other side was grass, then there were more of the silvery roadways, but this time between high walls of the tallest buildings we had ever seen, and at each level, bright lights shone from the windows. Here between the tall houses, it was quiet, with a faint sound of the passing vehicles nearby. There were no people, just deep shadows beneath the bright lights; our soft shoes padded in the near silence. 'Where can the populace be,' asked Odo, 'who will help us find hope from plague?'

'You won't get no help here,' a small voice intoned. We spun round and were confronted by a small boy, no more than seven or eight years old. His tiny face was smeared with dirt, and he was dressed in rags from which his thin arms and legs protruded, his feet covered in tied-up cloths. He held one hand to his ear, and mumbled constantly. 'What you doing here anyway?' The boy suddenly asked out loud.

'We need help,' Odo pleaded, 'for our village of Farnesleigh, we have the plague.'

'What's a plague?'

'Where are your parents?' I asked, 'where are the grown ups?'

'We're orphans,' the boy explained, 'we live in here.' He opened a darkened doorway into one of the buildings surrounding us. We followed him in. We were in a great gloomy cavern of a room, lit only in places by low white light from lamps. The vast room was filled with what looked like rubbish, piled upon trash and stinking things. On the piled up waste sat many boys and girls of different ages, all dressed much as the first boy we had encountered. All were mumbling into their hands which they held to their ear.

'We are from our village which has the plague,' Odo said, 'we need help. All of our people are dying. We have no food or water.'

'We cannot help you,' cried one of the many children, this time a girl of ten or eleven, 'the families, that is children with parents, live in the inner city, we orphans live here, we steal, we scavenge. We can give you beer and bread, but then you must go. If you are caught out in the city streets, the authorities take you away and you are never heard from again. You must go, even with your plague, you are better off there than here.'

They gave us bread which we ate, and opened round metallic containers which they said contained beer, but it was fizzy and bubbly and tasted disgusting, we could not drink it. 'And why,' I asked, 'do you all talk to yourself by mumbling into your hand?'

'They are communicators,' explained the boy, 'we talk to our friends. Let each other know when the authorities are around.' He held out his hand and we saw for the first time a communicator, a small, thin oblong with a tiny window. A voice came from the communicator, in a mumbled sound.

'I'll get one for you,' the boy said.

The children led us from the city back to the silver roadway that we crossed earlier, here we re-crossed back to the grass on the other side, and there the boy gave me one of the communicators. We marched on, and when we looked back the children were gone. We continued on up into the hills of the forest.

We found the tunnels, and eventually got back into the crypt of our church. The city of the children that we had visited was horrible. Odo and I are going back into the village, whatever our troubles are, we want to face them here, and not in the city. I keep with me, as a talisman of good luck, the communicator that the boy gave to me, he said it is called a mobile fone.'

'No! No!' Bernard Hughes cried, 'a mobile phone! It cannot be!' He grabbed the brittle, brown and faded paper and its bag from the desk. It crackled and fell to pieces on the floor, spilling from its interior a black oblong shape with what looked like keys on its side. The black shape disintegrated into dust as it rattled to the floor

---

Beyond Belief
To defy or go beyond what is believable.

ME FIRST!

The little beige four door saloon car buzzed along in the left hand lane of the motorway, a cars length away from the massive back of a truck in front and followed closely behind by another enormous truck. In fact when the driver of the little beige car, Glenda, looked in her mirror, all she could see was the massive radiator grill of the big truck bearing down threateningly right behind her. Glenda hated driving on the motorways but as she had been visiting her aunt in the north of England, the quickest way of returning to the south was on the terrifying motorways.

Glenda took a quick look in the mirror to see how her two daughter's were getting on in the back, hoping that they were settling down for the long journey home. The first image in the reflection was her own; shortish blonde hair, hazel eyes, short nose, shining white teeth and pale lipstick, thin white cardigan with black trousers and leather shoes. Then her eyes flicked to the back seats, where her girls were sitting in their places looking bored: Emma who was eight and Sarah, ten, both pretty with dark hair, dark eyes and pink complexions, both wearing multi coloured cardigans, long red leggings and trainers.

'Are we nearly there yet Mum,' Emma asked, with a yawn, 'is it a long way?'

'No, of course we're not there yet,' Glenda snapped back, trying to sound angry, 'we've got a long way to go still, we've got to drive down to the south of the country, we've been in the north, visiting aunty Mary haven't we?'

'Can't we get a bigger car? Or at least one with a DVD player?' Sarah complained, 'and I could do with a drink,' she said, giving a good rendition of a dry cough. 'And what's that horrible buzzing noise?'

Glenda looked down to the dash board of the car, a look of horror on her face. 'Oh, no!' she cried as she saw the "low fuel" light and heard the warning buzzer. She hadn't even thought to fill up the gas tank before she left aunt Mary's town.

And now she was on a busy motorway and running low on petrol!

As if on cue, the sky filled with heavy, black clouds and large drops of rain smacked on the windscreen. 'Look for a service station,' Glenda instructed the girls, 'we'll fill up with petrol there and be on our way home again.'

'We just passed service station,' giggled Sarah, 'not two minutes ago.'

'That means that there won't be another turn off to Services for miles and miles then,' snorted Emma, 'we'll run out of petrol on the motorway.'

'No we won't,' insisted Glenda, 'we'll turn off at the next junction, find a petrol garage, fill up and re-join the motorway later.' They drove on, and on, in the seemingly endless lane, the truck behind looming threateningly closer and closer, while the spray from the back of the truck in front was masking any signposts until it was too late to see a turn off. And all the while, the low fuel light flickered ominously, each time with a quick sound from the buzzer making them all jump as the sky darkened and the rain began to fall heavily. Glenda flicked a switch, and the windscreen wipers began their swishing, back and forth.

'There's a turn!' Quick!' the girls cried together, pointing to a signpost which read: EAST DIBBIN, 'turn off here.'

'But that's not for Services,' said Glenda, 'it's just a turn off for a small town or village... still, I'd better take it, we don't want to run out of petrol on the motorway.' She flicked on her left hand signal, and moved into the slip lane, as the big truck behind seemed to roar and thunder even closer to her back bumper as she left the motorway lane.

They followed the narrow road which led away down from the roaring motorway along a leafy lane towards a roundabout at the bottom where there were no signposts showing the way to the town or village of East Dibbin. Down one of the lanes leading from the roundabout, Glenda saw the roof of a house and turned towards that. 'If this is a tiny place with no shops,' Glenda said to herself, 'we're in trouble. I've just got to get petrol.'

'And a drink,' Sarah said in a mutter, 'and if we've got such a long way to go, can I buy some comics as well?'

They drove slowly on in silence – except for the occasional buzz from the fuel gauge – the lane was lined with green bushes and tall trees, and just a lonely house or two. Then further on, more houses and a shop appeared. 'This must be it!' Glenda cried, 'there's a shop, and it's called East Dibbin Stores...'

'And it's closed,' Emma noted as she saw the blinds over the door of the establishment. They drove further on and the old fashioned country houses, with their tiled roofs and wooden gates, were now lining either side of the lane and with a butcher's shop, a newsagent, and a post office, things were looking up.

'There! At last,' Glenda announced with relief, 'a petrol station.' Just at the end of the little village they could see through the rain a tiny forecourt and one bright red petrol pump under a small canopy. 'Wow, that's a relief,' sighed Glenda, 'we've got long way to go, all the way down south, we'd better fill right up.'

Just as she was to turn in to the entrance of the little garage, a man in rumpled blue overalls and a baseball cap pulled a chain across the entrance to the petrol station. 'What's up?' Glenda asked as she pulled up beside him, while her heart sank in anticipation that something was very wrong.

He was an old man with grey hair sprouting out of the sides of the baseball cap he wore, with a lined face and dark eyes, a long nose and wet lips. 'No petrol, luv, 'cos the delivery tanker can't get through the traffic which is jammed in another village,' the man said holding the chain, 'well, we have got *some* fuel, but the card machine 's broke, so you can't pay by card, it's cash only, so the area boss phoned and told me to close up.'

'Quick, girls,' Glenda whispered over her shoulder, 'look sad for the man.' Emma and Sarah both began to sob and cry theatrically in the back of the little car. 'Oh, please,' Glenda continued, 'can't we get just *some* petrol? We've got such a long way to go down south.'

'Oh, umm...' the old boy looked at the girls in the back and said, 'well, I could let you have *some* petrol, I reckon.' He returned the chain onto its hook and went back in his little kiosk and switched on the lighting for the petrol station.

Glenda hoped that the man would believe her, when she told him that she had no cash, in fact, she was absolutely broke but would owe him the money for the petrol she was going to take. She didn't want to deceive him really, but she had her daughters to get home safely, and her credit card was empty anyway.

As Glenda made her way forward to the pump, a large black saloon car reversed into the petrol station from the other end, the end marked: Exit. The car reversed right up to the only petrol pump, a big man got out and slid alongside his car up to the nozzle of the pump. He was a big, heavily built man in a dark blue suit, the collar of his white shirt was open where a loosened black tie hung, he had dark unruly hair, staring brown eyes, and a thick nose on his dark complexioned face. He sneered a lopsided grin.

'The man said I could have petrol...' Glenda stammered as she got out of her car and started to unscrew the filler cap.

'Well,' stated the man with a threatening look, 'after me, you're first.' He grabbed the petrol hose from the pump and turned to open the filler on his car. Glenda noted that he had to hold on to the side of the car as he did so, and that was when she could whiff the strong smell of alcohol oozing off the man.

'But there's not a lot of petrol left in this garage,' pleaded Glenda, 'and I've got to travel to the south of England with my two girls...'

'Yeah,' he said with a glassy look in his eye, as he plunged the hose into his filler, 'and I'm going a long way north. So you've got no option but to wait for me.' He laughed, swaying slightly as he pulled the trigger on the hose and began to fill his car with petrol. Glenda fumed helplessly as she stared into the back of his drunken head as he turned away.

As he held the nozzle into the filler of his car, with his

other hand he delved into his inside jacket pocket and withdrew a very large wad of £20 notes, held together by a rubber band, ready to pay for his petrol. 'Mum,' Emma asked from the back of Glenda's car, 'has that man just got a bacon roll from his pocket?'

'No it aint.' The man turned his head and snapped at the girls, 'it's more money than you'll ever see, just stay where you are and shut up!'

It seemed to take forever to fill his tank, but at last he stopped, and handed the filler hose to Glenda. 'Here,' he laughed, breathing a beery breath into Glenda's face, 'put this back for me, there's a good girl.' he laughed.

'What?' Glenda fumed even more at the arrogant, smug-faced idiot laughing at her.

'Put the hose back in the pump for me, dahlin,' he insisted, 'if you don't, the little man in the office won't know how much to charge me, and you won't get to find out if there's any petrol left for you. Now, put the hose back.' He thrust the hose painfully into Glenda's hand.

For one brief moment, as he staggered drunkenly away, Glenda was tempted to throw down the hose and drive out, but she really did have a long way to drive south, and both the girls were now at the point of crying, after he had so threateningly shouted at them. She re-seated the hose.

After a long wait, the pump clicked and gurgled, and re-set itself ready for the next customer. Glenda started to fill her little car, hoping with every gurgle of the flowing petrol did not mean that it had run out.

'That's done then,' the man said as he arrived back to his car after paying for his petrol, 'I'm all done, got enough gas to take me where I want to go, might even stop for a couple of pints on the way as well. An' if you run out of gas on your way south, have a nice night.' He laughed as he pulled open his jacket and thrust in the still-large wad of notes, jumped into his car and roared off, out of the petrol station, out of the village and into the motorway traffic, he was gone for good.

As Glenda finished filling her car — and there was just enough in the pump to do so — the garage man re-hung the chain on the Entrance end of the petrol station to close up for the day. When she had finished with the hose, Glenda hung up the nozzle and turned to go to the office to hopefully explain about her inability to pay, she stepped onto something on the ground by her car.

'Oh, what's that?' Glenda asked, looking down, as she lifted up her foot.

'That bacon roll fell out of the man's pocket,' the girls cried with a giggle as Glenda lifted up the wad of £20 notes in the rubber band.

The man had disappeared, vanished into thin air, and dived into the traffic, they could never find him again, no matter how they searched. Glenda looked down at the roll of banknotes in her hand, then at the little window where the garage man waited for her to pay cash.

Vanish into thin air

To go without trace

WINNER TAKES ALL

The slate grey Rolls-Royce limousine slowed down as it glided along the country lane, then swung left and stopped before a pair of tall black painted, wrought iron gates, set into a high stone wall which stretched in either direction of the long lane. The driver, a young man in a peaked cap and smart grey uniform, with white shirt and red tie, reached into his jacket pocket for his mobile phone, pressed a small set of numbers on it and pocketed the phone while he waited for the phone's signal to work. Almost instantly, the iron gates in front of the car began to open. He gently oozed the car forward through the gates and watched in his interior mirror as they automatically closed behind him. The car wafted gently along the half mile long driveway and eventually stopped in front of the main door of Moorland Forest Mansion.

The Moorland Forest Mansion, one of the largest privately owned mansions in the country, traced its history back to the fifteenth century, when the country changed from the royal family of York to that of the Tudors. The first great house being on this site, or so historians said, was gifted to a fighting knight as the spoils of war, as in those days, the winners of a great battle would take everything they could from their defeated foes.

In those medieval times, the wealth, lands, wives, army, servants, villages and their populations, goods and gold, all were taken by the victors of a battle. And that they say was how Moorland Forest Mansion was once acquired; in 1485 when Henry Tudor became King Henry VII of England after his victorious battle of Bosworth Field when he defeated King Richard III, and gave the mansion to a faithful warrior-knight as a gift.

The great mansion had been improved and enlarged over the many hundreds of years since, its great hall became a massive banqueting hall, its outer buildings grew, its stabling became immense, its rooms and kitchens enlarged to enormous sizes. Then in the eighteenth century, it completely outgrew itself.

Moorland Forest Mansion became too big, too expensive to maintain, its servants and staff too costly to maintain. It closed.

Then in the present day came along Michael Simon Newcomen, entrepreneur, landowner, railway owner, airline owner and oil refining multi billionaire, who bought the massive place for an undisclosed fortune as a headquarters for his business enterprises and a palatial home for himself, staff and family. He had sent his private secretary, John Hood, to organise the refurbishment – indeed the tearing out of anything old – of the ancient buildings to convert it into a modern day wonder home/palace.

As soon as the Rolls-Royce stopped at the small flight of stone steps below the main double door entrance to the Mansion, John Hood skipped down the stairs and opened the passenger door for his boss. John Hood was tall and slim, had white hair which was kept short, intense dark eyes, thin nose, wide toothy smile and an air of confidence, he was as usual, immaculately turned out in slim fitting faintly striped blue suit with waistcoat, white shirt, black tie and black shoes which positively shone. 'Hello, Michael,' he said brightly to the man, his employer, in the rear passenger seat, 'welcome to your new home, Moorland Forest Mansion. Be careful, there are workmen everywhere, refurbishing, renewing and rebuilding. It's going to be great.'

Michael Simon Newcomen stepped from the car. He was a lot younger than his private secretary, had dark hair, bright brown eyes and a smile on his handsome, clean shaven, tanned face. He wore an open necked yellow shirt below a "v" necked grey jumper, blue trousers and soft brown shoes. 'Thanks, John,' he answered his secretary, as they ascended the stairs together, 'I'd just like to take a look around, get the feel of the place.' Michael Newcomen was a hard-headed businessman, but in his private time, he was a calm, unpretentious person.

Together they walked the great halls and corridors of the Mansion, as John explained what the many workmen were doing, how it was being rebuilt and refurbished and double glazed, as they skirted their way around the many overall wearing workers, who were preparing stonework, stripping paperwork from walls, painting and building, working everywhere in the great house.

Soon the two parted as Michael did what he had come for; to wander the great house and watch its rebirth. He watched some men rebuilding a wooden arch into the banqueting hall; stood in front of a large window and watched the gardeners outside, digging up the grounds for replanting flower beds.

He wandered the great house and soon found himself in a lower corridor with stone flagged floor and walls, with just a few temporary swinging electric lights strung from the ceiling. At the other end of the long hall, a woman appeared, and walked purposefully towards him. Michael did not know this woman, which was not unusual; he could not know all the staff who worked for his vast enterprises.

The woman was about thirty years old with thick, long black hair which flowed down her back, a beautiful opalesque white face with sparkling blue eyes, long eyelashes, sharp nose and a set look on her attractive mouth, all on a face that had no make-up. She wore a gold coloured, unbuttoned long coat which flowed behind her showing a low cut blouse and knee length skirt. She looked fantastic, he thought, as she walked towards him, her white skin seeming to light up the dim corridor.

'Hello,' he said as they closed in on one another, and he stopped, 'I'm afraid I don't know...'

'How dare you,' she turned on him, showing gleaming white teeth, 'how dare you disturb my son after all this time.' She continued to walk on down the corridor, and turned her head to continue as she went, her black hair flowing behind her, 'leave him. Leave him I say!'

'But who are you?' he asked in surprise, as he stood and watched her walk on.

'Elizabeth Woodville.' she called back as Michael watched fascinated as she disappeared into the gloomy shadows formed by the flickering, swinging electric lights.

'Sir! Sir!' someone called from the other end of the

corridor. Michael looked at the caller; a young man wearing a white shirt and blue jeans covered in a long grey apron, it was one of the excavation men who were working on the lower parts of the building which were being opened up for the first time in many hundreds of years.

'What is it?' Michael asked the excited man, slightly put out at being called away from the beautiful woman who had so petulantly walked on.

'We've made a discovery,' answered the man breathlessly, beckoning Michael to follow him, 'we were at one of the lowest places in the Mansion, deep underground, where we found a box of something, we thought that you would want to be there when it is opened.' The two hurried on, the young man leading the way, and at the end of the corridor they turned into a small doorway and clattered down a stone staircase lit by more hanging bulbs, where the air became cold.

At the bottom of the stairs was a small square room where another of the young men wearing an apron over his street clothes waited. The room was made of large grey-blue flagstones, it had stone flagged walls, ceiling and floor, and was empty except for a wooden casket on the floor, which had been taken from behind one of the wall stones which was gaping open. 'When we entered this room, I noted that one of the stones was loose,' said the young man who had led Michael there, 'and this is what we found behind it.' He pointed to the casket.

Michael hunched down and looked at the casket, it was indeed ancient. It was made of wood, which was old and green, with rusty metal hinges. It looked to be about one metre long and over half a metre wide by less than half a metre deep. Through a gap in the old wood, near a metal hinge, Michael could see what looked like some ancient, threadbare clothing and what looked like charred pieces of bone.

'There is a story in the written history of Moorland Forest Mansion,' continued the young man, 'it seems that the owner of the mansion, Thomas Woodville, fought on the losing side of an ancient battle and was killed. The new king gave this mansion to one of his knights, Gawayn Faulkes, who had fought fiercely for him at the battle, as a gift after defeating the enemy. When the knight Faulkes got here he found that Thomas Woodville's wife had a new born baby son, and although Faulkes, by the new King's order, was the new and legal lord of the manor, he saw the young Woodville baby and the heredity of the child as a threat to his new status, so had killed the boy, by throwing him onto the fire, in the lower parts of the Mansion, which I think is where this box was sealed. It seems the woman – Woodville's wife - fought Faulkes tooth and nail to save the boy, fighting with all her might, punching, kicking and clawing like a mad woman to save her child's life, but to no avail; in the end she was defeated by a strong, fighting fit knight.

The boy's mother hid the child's remains and his clothes in a box and had it sealed into one of the fireplaces behind some stone flaggings here, and then she disappeared from history, but rumour has it that for the rest of her life she haunted this mansion, guarding the remains of her son. She had been a beautiful and powerful woman, apparently she had long thick black hair which flowed down her back, a beautiful white clear-skinned face with sparkling blue eyes. Her name was...'

'Elizabeth Woodville,' interrupted Michael Newcomen, 'I think I just met her. Have this box re-closed and seal it back into place in the wall. We must never open it again.'

Get Medieval

Use violence or extreme measures.

London Bridge

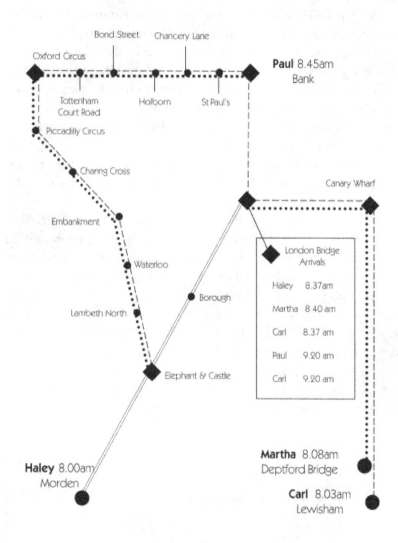

Bond Street   Chancery Lane

Oxford Circus

Tottenham
Court Road   Holborn   St Paul's

Paul 8.45am
Bank

Piccadilly Circus

Charing Cross

Canary Wharf

Embankment

London Bridge
Arrivals

Waterloo

Haley   8.37am

Borough

Martha   8.40 am

Lambeth North

Carl   8.37 am

Paul   9.20 am

Carl   9.20 am

Elephant & Castle

Martha 8.08am
Deptford Bridge

Haley 8.00am
Morden

Carl 8.03am
Lewisham

LONDON BRIDGE

8.00am, Morden, Surrey.
Haley Linneman stepped onto the Northern Line underground train at Morden Station. The train she boarded was a "Bank" line train, not a "Charing Cross" line train, as the Northern line splits at Kennington station, and Haley's destination was London Bridge station on the Bank line.

Haley was a slim sixteen year old with chin-length blond hair, hazel eyes in her lightly made up face, and a wide smile showing white teeth. She wore a red cardigan, tight black trousers and leather sandals, and carried with her a large brown cloth bag held with a strap over her shoulder. Her left hand held tightly on top of the bag, as it was holding something very valuable.

Usually at Morden, which is the last station at the southern end of the Northern Line, it was easy to get a seat, but at this time in the morning, there was a crowd of people on the platform mostly heading off to work in London, and Haley elbowed and shoved her way to a seat. She sat and held the bag tightly to her, as the push of the crowd barged in to get a place to sit.

As the train pulled out of Morden station it was full, with men and women, now that the seats were all taken, standing near the doors and in the aisles, hanging onto the overhead hand-straps, while uniformed school children giggled while they squeezed along the carriage around the other passengers, as the train picked up speed. Haley had looked forward to this day for the last two and a half weeks, when her mum had collapsed at the office where she worked, just across London Bridge and had been taken by ambulance to the Guy's Hospital Casualty.

The hospital had been performing exploratory procedures to try to find out what was wrong with her mum, who had been having a painful tummy for some time. But yesterday Haley had been told that the doctors and staff had found what was wrong, and her mum could be treated safely at home in future.

Now that she was coming home, mum had instructed Haley to bring her up to the hospital some make up, jewellery and credit card to pay for a taxi home from the hospital and to pay for food shopping on the way. Haley hadn't been able to find the credit card so had taken the £50 cash from the tin in the kitchen that her mum kept for emergencies and added £60 that Haley had in a jar in her bedroom. This cash, plus her mum's jewellery were all in the tightly held bag she had on her lap.

At the next stop, South Wimbledon, even more passengers squeezed onto the train. Haley didn't notice the extra crush of people jamming in the carriage, because she was so pleased! She had always relied on her mum for everything, and had felt completely lost without her. Her mum looked after the housework, shopping, finances and cooking. Haley had had enough of cola and microwave fries for dinner while her mum was away, and doing her own washing and ironing, and the milk for her corn flakes in the morning was definitely slightly whiffy.

Suddenly the doors of the carriage whizzed open. Colliers Wood station already! A few more people crammed on, into the stuffy atmosphere of the carriage, then the doors zoomed closed and they were off again. After that, Haley went into a sort of half awake doze, one of those times when a traveller on the tube just has to wait, to let the stations pass by, as the train rattled along on its way into central London. Some of the passengers read newspapers or books, some stared into space, and some took sly looks at their fellow passengers, and decided what kind of person they were.

The train moved on, buzzing noisily away on its busy journey, stopping here and there, passengers cramming themselves in, or fighting the crowds at different stops to try and push past people to get out onto the platform at their stop. It became very warm in the carriages, and Haley felt herself nodding off as the train rocked back and forth along the rails.

'Oh,' she thought as she jerked awake, 'what station was that? Was I asleep? Was that last station London Bridge?' She stared through the window on the opposite side of the carriage at the last of the station name plaques as the train sped out of the station. 'No,' she thought gratefully, as she read the station name, 'it was Clapham North.' She drearily watched the next stops go by, making sure she didn't fall asleep, clutching firmly onto to her bag. Then further on, it was Oval station, then Kennington, Elephant and Castle, Borough – London Bridge! At last. It's the next stop!

At 8.37am the train arrived at London Bridge, at Platform One of the Northern Line.

Haley struggled up from her seat, as did half of the passengers - this was a very important stop - and everyone hung onto the overhead straps and shuffled to the nearest door. With a jerk, the train suddenly stopped and all the lined-up people were thrown forward onto the person in front. Then there was the dash forward, as the doors swished open and the mass exit started, as a great crowd of people rushed for the doors.

Just as Haley turned at the end of the seating to exit the carriage, she was pushed from behind by the crowd, and her sandal strap caught in the high heel of the young lady in front of her. Caught with just one foot on the floor of the train and being bumped from behind, Haley fell forward, half out of the carriage. She fell onto her face, her forehead banging the concrete of the station platform. Her lights went out.

New Cross Road, Deptford

Martha Strudman was seventy seven years old and *tired*, her legs ached and her arms ached, but she was a worker, had always worked, and would continue to work, it was her life. Her working day had started at six o'clock this morning as it did every day.

Martha was small and thin, her greying hair was held back by a strong clip, and she wore pink framed bi-focal glasses in front of her brown eyes. Her freckled face was creased with laughter lines, as she seemed to have a weary smile for everyone. She wore a square necked blue jumper under a grey coat with black trousers and slip-on black shoes.

Martha hated going to the pub each day, where she was now, and cleaning and dusting, she felt that she was too old and the work was too tiring, but the landlord of the pub had been friends with Martha's husband, and paid her in cash for her work, and today was a special day: it was her twin grandson's fourteenth birthday and she had arranged to meet them on Platform One at London Bridge underground station and take them to Borough Market for a walk along the Thames riverside and then they could have whatever food they wanted from the market. The food that was cooked and sold at the market was always a great treat and the boys, she knew, would love it.

On impulse, Martha opened her bright red purse, with its distinctive silver dragon motif on its side and checked that she had the £100 in notes that she had put in there for the boys' day out, it was all safely in there, so she stuffed the purse on top of her shopping bag, which had some tea towels in that she was going to wash for the pub kitchen.

She had left her tiny one bedroom flat at 5.30am and had stepped carefully down the too-steep staircase to the ground floor where she had walked out onto the street. She then trudged down two empty roads, then unlocked and entered the door into *The Crown and Anchor* pub, and started cleaning the bar, the toilets and the chairs and tables, just as she did every day. Two hours later, at 8.00am, Martha let herself out of the empty pub as she closed and locked the outer door and strode away towards the Docklands Light Railway station.

8.08am Deptford Bridge station.

Martha stepped onto the DLR train, and as usual there were no vacant seats, the train was full of passengers at this busy time in the morning, so she gave a shrug and stood by the window. She stared out of the speeding carriage as the stations drifted by, hardly aware of her surroundings. After a jerky stop at Canary Wharf at 8.20am, Martha lifted her weary feet and alighted from the train onto Platform Six, completely unaware that her purse had been stolen from her shopping bag. Martha trudged along with the other passengers, and joined the rush of travellers down the steps, and out, across the road, into the Underground station to the Jubilee Line, Platform One, to go to London Bridge.

A few minutes after standing with the other people on the crowded platform, a tube train arrived and Martha stepped on for the quick three stops to London Bridge.

As soon as she got out of the train at London Bridge station, Martha went up the stairs to the Northern Line platform to meet her twin grandson's. She arrived at Platform One at 8.40am but all she saw was a gathering of people around a poor girl who was lying in a heap on the ground. Martha went over to see if she could help.

8.03am, Lewisham station

Carl Beresford stepped onto the Docklands Light Railway driverless train with a crowd of people, all heading in towards Canary Wharf. Carl was aged twenty three, had dark hair shaved close to his scalp, brown eyes, a sharp nose on his dusky skinned face with a thin moustache and beard. He wore a black round-necked T-shirt under a brown three-quarter length coat and dark blue jeans and black trainers. He looked like any other young man going to work on the early train. Which was exactly what Carl wanted; to mix invisibly in with the crowd, because Carl was a thief and pickpocket and this was his daily work. But Carl had to be careful, he was known to the police as he'd been caught before, and had to be alert, always looking out warily for the Old Bill.

Carl had never known who his father was and had lived with his mum in a tiny two bedroomed flat until he had finished school, when he had left home for good. He now "dossed" in a broken down flat where a dozen or more young people slept, all chipping in a bit of money to pay the rent with no questions asked.

He let the crowd surge onto the train before him, he

didn't want to sit down, he wanted to mingle with the passengers pressed together near the doors. By the time they had reached Mudchute Station the train was full, and Carl went to work...

There by the door was an old girl gazing out of the window with her shopping bag gaping open beside her, and inside the shopping bag on top of the goods: a purse! a bright red purse, with a picture of a silver dragon on its side. As the train rattled on, Carl slowly inched himself nearer to his mark, always seeming to look the other way, gently shuffling by other people on the crowded carriage. He relieved one man of a very expensive-looking pen from his top pocket, and took a folded banknote from the cardigan pocket of a scruffy looking young man, then he was by the old girls side. The train stopped at Cross Harbour, then went on to South Quay. As they pulled away from that station, Carl noticed the old girl straighten up. Now was the time! She seemed to be preparing to exit the train at the next stop. Carl readied himself. At Heron Quays, the old girl just shuffled forward as the doors opened, then relaxed. With a heightening tension Carl knew that she was getting off at the next stop, Canary Wharf. Soon the train doors hissed closed and they were off again.

Then quite quickly the train slowed down with a jerk as it entered Canary Wharf station; Carl fell forward, holding out his left hand to stop himself bumping into the old girl. Distracted, as she looked right up at him, his right hand shot down into her bag and took the purse, sliding it quickly into his coat pocket. The train stopped. The doors opened. The old girl got out onto the platform with the other passengers and walked off. Carl gave as long as possible for the old dear to disappear into the crowd, then, just as the carriage doors began to close Carl jumped out and sauntered across the platform. It was 8.26am.

Carl wandered around the station and then followed the surge of people down the stairs, left onto the main concourse to Cabot Place, then right through the doors to the street, still milling in with the crowd, looking for another mark, a lost soul or just someone having a problem of some sort, for him to rob. Then he nipped across the road, and down into the Canary Wharf Underground Station to the Jubilee Line.

He got on the first train that came in, his working day had just begun. He watched the passengers in the carriage, looking for an easy mark. Canada Water station came and went, then in a few minutes they arrived at Bermondsey, but the people on this train seemed alert and awake, not what he was looking for at all, so he jumped onto the platform at the next stop, London Bridge.

He wandered to his right, then left through the exit, up the stairs mixing with the milling passengers and arrived on the Northern Line Platform One at 8.37am. A train thundered into the station and came to a stop, and as soon as the doors opened, a thousand people poured from the open doors. And what was that? A young girl came falling headlong out of the doors and crashed onto the platform, knocking herself out. Her bag went tumbling along the floor.

Without stopping, Carl swept up the bag, rolled it up in its shoulder strap and stuffed it into his coat pocket with the old girls purse from the earlier train, then kept walking swiftly along the platform as far as he could to its end where he jumped into the first carriage of the still waiting train. All the while behind him, a small group of people gathered around the fallen girl who had tumbled out of the train. Once inside the front carriage he stood in the corner by the door and stuffed the bag he had just stolen further down into his pocket. At the next station, which was Bank, Carl got off the train onto the platform.

8.45am Bank Station, Platform One.

Among the people waiting on the platform at Bank Station was a tall black man, Paul Heddon. Paul was 35, tall and muscular with a shaven head, intense dark eyes, slim moustache and stubbly beard. He was dressed in a mauve shirt, black leather waistcoat, blue jeans and scuffed white trainers. A draw-string bag hung on his back from his shoulders, which held his paperwork, torch, pepper spray, window punch and handcuffs. Paul Heddon was a Transport Police officer, working undercover.

As the passengers from the last train exited the platform, Paul's mental index of known criminals was alerted. A face. Paul had seen that face before. Casually turning, he followed. The young man he pursued had dark hair, brown eyes, dusky skin and a thin moustache and beard, wearing a dark T-shirt and a brown three-quarter length coat, jeans and trainers.

Paul followed a fair way behind, as they turned right towards the end of the platform, then up the stairs and straight on to the Central Line, and on up the spiral staircase to Platform Five on the Central Line going west. As the man mixed with the passengers on the platform, Paul tried to put a name to the face. As the next train clattered into the station and the man got on, followed by Paul in the next carriage, Paul thought: 'Charlie...? Cal...? Chris...? Carl! Yes, that's it. Carl.'

The stations passed as Paul observed the man. First they passed Saint Paul's station, then Chancery Lane. 'Beresford!' Paul thought happily, 'that's him, Carl Beresford. He's a known criminal who travels the London Underground picking people's pockets.' In among the other passengers in the next carriage where Paul could see him, Carl suddenly looked round as though aware of someone watching him. He looked straight at Paul through the sea of faces and the glass of the interconnecting door of the two carriages. Their eyes met.

'Oh, no,' Carl thought, 'Old Bill! And I've got two nicked bags on me!' As the train pulled in at the next stop, Holborn, and the people began to leave the train, Carl dashed for the exit just as the doors began to close. Paul was ready to follow. But Carl stopped on the train at the last moment, as the doors began to close. The train travelled on.

At Tottenham Court Road station Carl seemed to hunch down and mingle with the crowd but again did not leave the train. The next stop was Oxford Circus and here Carl *did* leave the train in amid the other travellers and turned left and on to the Bakerloo Line Platform Three, where Carl jumped onto a train with Paul hot on his tail.

On this train, as soon as they had begun to move, Carl, with a backward glance at Paul, moved through the crowd and opened the door to the next carriage while the train was in motion. Paul followed. They swiftly passed Piccadilly Circus, Charing Cross and Embankment stations. At the next stop, Waterloo, Carl got off the train and began to walk with others, down the platform towards the sign for Way Out. Paul followed, 'this guy's walking too near to the open doors of the train,' Paul said to himself, and sure enough, just as the doors began to close Carl jumped back on board the train again. The train moved off, and although Paul was still on the train, he was now two carriages away.

At Lambeth North station, Paul jumped out onto the platform and ran forward, quickly diving into the next open door. This time he was in the same carriage as Carl, and Paul began to push his way forward, through the passengers as the train stopped in Elephant and Castle, where Carl ran from the train down the platform. Paul ran after him, and Carl made it to the Northern Line platform just as the doors were closing on a Bank train. Carl jumped on and Paul made it onto the carriage behind.

They were off again. This time Paul was not going to miss out. He began to work his way through the crowded train to the next carriage. Then it was Borough station and Carl, hanging onto an overhead strap, took a slow look behind himself, hoping that the copper was gone, but was surprised to see him standing directly behind him. 'Carl,' Paul held firmly onto Carl's arm, 'don't make a fuss, or I'll hold you down and cuff you on the train.'

'Look, I haven't done anything wrong,' said Carl, wild eyes looking around for a way out, 'I've paid my oyster card.'

'Just wait until the next stop,' ordered Paul, 'I'll search you there, if you're not holding anything, you can go. But, you know, it's about time you thought of your future. Is this what you are going to do for the rest of your life? And keep getting caught and spend most of your time in prison?'

At 9.20am the train pulled in at London Bridge station, Northern Line, and on the platform, right where their door opened, a small gathering of people still stood over the still groggy figure of Haley Linneman who was sitting on the floor with a bumped head, being looked after by Martha Strudman and a few other concerned people who stood around trying to help.

Carl made up his mind in a moment. He snatched his arm from Paul's grasp and ran for it. At that time, someone standing around the fallen girl moved to one side and Carl smashed into him, sending them both sprawling to the ground. Haley's leather bag tumbled out of Carl's pocket onto the floor with Martha's bright red purse, with its distinctive silver dragon picture. 'Oh, there's my bag,' Haley said gratefully, 'I don't want to lose that.' She sat up with a dizzy smile.

'Ooh, I must have dropped my purse as well,' said Martha, stuffing her purse back into her shopping bag.

Paul dragged Carl up from the midst of the people on the platform and searched him. 'Well, I can't find anything on you,' he said wistfully, 'you can go.'

'Thanks,' responded Carl with a sigh as he dusted himself off, 'and you're right, I just might think of a change of occupation. I've never fancied working for a living, but after today I think I'd better bite the bullet, and I'll face the future better, with an honest life.'

Bite the Bullet
Accept the inevitable impending hardship
and endure the result with fortitude.

EMPIRE

The enormous silvery white spaceship, *Earth Endeavour* silently floated in from outer space, then settled into orbit above the deep-blue planet. This would be the first new world visited by mankind, it would be Earth's first contact. Using conventional rocketry, it would take seventy-six thousand years for a vehicle to reach Earth's nearest star in the next solar system, but this giant space ship was powered by super fast projectile engines with solar wind assistance allowing it to reach fantastic speeds, and had reached this planet in the nearest solar system to Earth in a mere fifty years.

On the *Endeavour's* arrival at the planet in the new solar system, the crew had been awakened from the deep cryogenic sleep that they had been induced into for the long journey, so they had slept in deep hibernation, not ageing a single day, until their arrival at a habitable planet.

Alpha Centauri, the nearest solar system to Earth's had at last been reached, and *Endeavour* hovered over the white cloud-covered blue planet. When they got their first view of the first Earth-like world that man had ever visited, someone on the team had cried: "Whassat?" and that had been used as the name for the planet down below them since that moment by the crew.

Sean Villiers, Captain of the *Endeavour* stood at the observation screen and marvelled at the view below. 'It's just like Earth,' he said quietly, 'just like Earth; it's about the same size as our planet and the gravity is identical to ours, and the air is *sooo* fresh.' Sean was, like the other three crew members of his super spaceship, tall, good looking and athletically built. He had dark, almost black, short hair which was tinged with grey, had dark eyebrows above soft brown eyes, and a straight nose on his tanned face, with a set mouth on a stubbly chin. He wore the uniform of the Space Federation of Planet Earth; short silver zip up top, long silver trousers and soft silver boots.

Behind Sean Villiers stood his similarly uniformed crew: Roberta Blandford, Navigator and Psychologist. Roberta was younger than her Captain at thirty-two years of age, tall with long blond hair, slim and shapely with grey eyes, golden skin and a natural smile on her make-up free face.

By her side was Cristiano Ford, Flight Engineer and Negotiator. Cristiano was a solidly built man in his middle thirties, a shaven headed black man with a full moustache and beard. All the three members of the super ship stared at the view screen.

The planet below was indeed beautiful; deeply blue oceans surrounded large and small islands seen in glimpses between the fluffy white clouds. All three looked in awe at the beauty below. 'Well,' said Sean at long last, 'we knew it was here, but we didn't know how much like Earth it was...'

'Or if it was inhabited,' Cristiano said without taking his eyes from the screen, 'can we tell yet?'

'And if it *is* inhabited,' mused Roberta, turning towards the Captain, 'what are the inhabitants like? Have they evolved to be just like us?'

'Well, we all know that the Earth is overpopulated,' Sean continued, 'our planet is so full of people, everywhere is overcrowded. In cities people live like tinned fish, packed into rooms, the deserts of our world are full of cardboard and corrugated iron shacks with no plumbing or electricity, the city roads and pavements are bursting with campsites full of crowds of people living in tents and wooden huts. We need a new world to populate. All we can hope is that if Whassat is inhabited, there is room for our people.'

'Let's send out a probe,' Cristiano suggested, 'we can programme it to search planet wide and find what the population, if any, is like.' Roberta moved forward to the console in front of them and pushed a multitude of buttons and very shortly, from a porthole in the side of *Endeavour* a small rocket powered torpedo flashed out and nose dived down towards the beautiful land of Whassat beneath the clouds below.

While they waited for the probe to circle the planet, the crew returned to the tasks of monitoring the workings of the giant ship *Endeavour*, checking on air and fuel recycling and reserves, food and general maintenance. While they busied themselves at their desks, they talked excitedly about the new planet Whassat below. 'I really hope that the planet isn't too fully populated,' Roberta said, 'it looks so clean and fresh.'

'Well, there's a string of giant spaceships which are to be people transporters being built in space that were orbiting the Earth when we left,' Cristiano said as he perused his readouts from the ships computer, 'if this planet is suitable, we can have millions of people here within fifty years. That'll take a bit of overcrowding off the Earth.'

'It all depends on what the probe brings back,' observed Captain Sean, 'If the population of Whassat below has evolved like ours, there could be people here. On the other hand, if the life on this planet evolved differently from us, the natives may be vastly different from us.'

'Yes, it all depends on evolution,' agreed Cristiano, 'I mean, on Earth when the many diverse life forms grew from pre-history, over millions of years, man didn't just evolve from an animal to a human. First there were the dead ends: the dinosaurs died out, as did the trilobites from at least five hundred million years ago, as did the micro-organisms that flourished and died. Some life forms ruled the Earth for millions of years and then died out.

'What modern man is, is the result of many life forms that have lived and died before us. We have inherited the results of many victories and failures of life. If any of the life forms that went before us had lived in mud or had wings, that may have been what we turned out to be. It's all to do with what was successful in life and what died out. We are the evolution of many living things that have made us the unique beings that we are.'

'So if there are people on this planet we have named Whassat,' asked Roberta, 'they may not be like us?'

'Exactly,' answered the Captain, 'we evolved from pre-history to the wild monkey to the cave man, to the human. If there are residents on Whassat, they may not be like us at all. They may have evolved from a different species altogether, and would be completely different from us.' Time passed, and the excited crew waited impatiently.

'Probe's pictures are in!' Roberta suddenly cried, punching buttons on her console, 'let's find out what it saw.' Once again the crew clustered around the viewscreen to see the findings of the probe, as it soared over Whassat's blue oceans and green continents. They gasped in pure joy as they saw schools of very large sea creatures arrowing through the open ocean, and saw herds of land animals roaming across open green countryside feeding on plants and tree fruits. 'Wait.' Captain Sean commanded, raising his hand, as Roberta pressed a pause button, 'a town. A town has appeared on screen. Or is it a city?' They all craned forward to look at the screen.

'It looks like a city,' said Cristiano sadly, 'I was hoping that Whassat would be uninhabited...'

'Yes, but look around the city,' Sean urged, 'look at the enormous open spaces surrounding the clustered city buildings.' As they all looked at the now continuing footage from the probe, they saw that there was indeed an immense amount of open space on the green planet.

'And look, look into the city,' Roberta cried as the probe continued on its way and they could see down into the city streets below, 'there's streets, and wheeled vehicles driving along, and movement on the pavements, but I just can't see what the natives look like down below...'

'We have to be prepared,' warned Sean, 'as I said before, we come from monkey and caveman forebears who lived thousands and thousands of years before we evolved. If the occupants of Whassat have evolved from a different species from us, they may be completely unlike us...'

'GREETINGS.' A deep commanding voice boomed from their loudspeakers, making everyone jump in surprise.

'What the...' Cristiano blurted, staggering back with sudden fright at the sound.

'Who's that?' Sean called out, looking around the flight deck in shock, 'who spoke?'

'Be calm, my friends, be calm,' the booming voice continued, 'when you arrived here at our planet, your speaker system was on, and we heard what you had to say. Sorry it took so long, but we had to learn your language from the words that you used, but now we can use your dialect and speak to you.

'Our planet is called Oovraya, and we are Oovrayans, not Whassats from Whassat.' the voice said with a hint of humour, 'and my name is Kadek, I am the leader of the world-wide family of Oovraya.'

'So you've been listening-in to us all the time?' Cristiano asked.

'Yes, we have,' answered the voice, 'we know that there is three of you in the ship, and that there is a great deal of energy and mechanical, nuclear fusion and fissionable material in the body of your vessel.'

'That's pretty good detection, Kadek,' Roberta replied, 'has Oovraya a space agency? Are you monitoring us? Are we in your gunsights?'

'No,' came Kadek's answer, 'we have some satellites, but no space ships or navy or armed forces of any kind. We have air travel, but no air *Force*. We live in peace with each other, and there are only four cities on Oovraya. We have known of your planet Earth's existence for many years...'

'But you've never tried to contact us?' Roberta asked, 'don't you have the technology to send a message all that way to the next solar system?'

'Yes, we have the technology,' answered Kadek, 'but you see... as you know, light is the fastest known thing, but light still takes time to travel. On planet Earth, the light from your Sun takes eight minutes and twenty seconds to reach to reach the surface of the planet.

'Now Oovraya is a *very* long way from Earth, but we

have observed your home planet in our telescopes. But the light from your planet takes a very, very long time to get here, so what we see of the planet Earth is actually pictures of your history, and at this time, all we can see is war. Your First World War, and now your Second World War.'

'But that's old history...' Cristiano protested, 'from way back in our planet's time.'

'Yes, it is old history,' insisted Kadek, 'but it is *your* history, monkey man. Here on Oovraya, we evolved, not from the chattering, aggressive, warlike monkey, but from creatures of the deep ocean. We are not aggressive or warlike. We watch in horror and disgust at how humans murder and kill each other for the possession of wealth, land and ownership, and the desire to be the overlord.'

'So, you think of us as beneath you,' snarled Sean, 'not as good as you.'

'No, no of course not,' Kadek continued, 'and now your world is overcrowded and worn out and you are looking for a new start for your race. We have been waiting for you to... settle down a bit, to lose some aggression. We welcome you, bring some of your people here and we will give them a home.'

'Well, as we may soon be neighbours,' Sean said, 'and if you've seen our history, you know what we look like, so how about meeting you?'

Suddenly the viewscreen went black, then flickered back into light. And the three crew members from Earth drew back in shock at what they saw.

On the screen Kadek appeared. His head was that of a grotesque fish face with bulging eyes and scaly flesh with bulbous lips. A thousand tiny tentacles writhed from his shoulders and many black, bone-like arms led from his silvery body down to three fingered, black bony hands. 'Well, hello Kadek,' Roberta said turning her face away from the screen in distaste.

'Look, Kadek,' Sean spoke up, 'we thank you for the opportunity to live on your planet. We, the people of Earth would bring you great wealth and success. Join us as part of the

Kingdom of Mankind...'

'Wait. Wait.' Kadek answered quickly, 'let's get this right; we don't want to join you. *You* want to join us. *You're* the one's asking for help. We have taken our time to watch your monkey man aggression, and we don't like it, and we do not crave wealth or success. We don't want to rule others, we already live well, and in peace. We don't want to join a force of humans who want to conquer and assimilate others, but you *can* join *us*... But we won't kowtow to you.'

Captain Sean turned to Roberta and drew his index finger across his throat in the silent message to cut the sound of Kadek and to silence the microphones on the *Endeavour's* flight deck, so that only the three could speak and hear each other. 'Well, now we know,' said Sean, 'they will only accept us as poor refugee immigrants.'

'They look down on us,' Cristiano spoke between clenched teeth.

'Monkey men,' Roberta laughed scornfully, 'they call us monkey men.'

'They will oppose us all the way,' Sean spoke harshly, 'I've decided how I feel: see if you agree. This ship has nuclear war fighting capabilities. I say we bomb the four cities of Oovraya, and send a message home to Earth: send five or six super ships full of our people out here, by the time they get here in fifty years time, the nuclear fall out contamination will have lifted and "monkey men" will have a new planet to populate.

Without answering, Roberta pressed all the right buttons and sent off four nuclear bombs.

Very soon the *Earth Endeavour* began to leave the stricken planet of Oovraya and sailed on into the blackness of space to its next destination, wherever that might be. And the three crew members went back into cryogenic sleep to await the great day.

To Kowtow to

To accept the authority of another;
to act in a subservient manner.

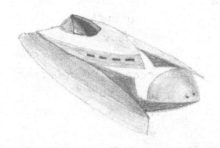

THE WARLORDS

The brick walls surrounding the old house were seven metres high with jagged, broken glass running along the top. A solid iron gate at the street side of the house slowly swung open inwardly to the sound of a rattling chain from inside the wall, where a dark haired woman with a tanned face looked out fearfully in each direction, as she turned the handle for the door chain. An old green Land Rover Defender with thick wire mesh guards covering all of its windows nosed its way out to the throbbing sound of its very powerful V8 engine. Large rusty iron sheets covered the vehicle's wheels to deflect arrows and bullets aimed at the tyres, and inside, two people sat in the front seats of the vehicle. Once out onto the street, after a signal from the driver, the chain began to rattle once again as the woman turned the handle on the chain's wheel and the iron gate swung closed. The Land Rover and its occupants were outside, in the bright, sunny morning.

The driver of the Land Rover was David Mortimer, a short, squat dark haired man in his forties with thick eyebrows over his brown eyes, a roundish pug nose, stubbly chin and wide mouth. He wore a black T-shirt under a short, multi pocketed jacket, and faded blue jeans with a brown leather belt, and black boots. The pockets of his jacket were stuffed full of ammunition for the holstered pistol hanging on his belt, and round his shoulder was a bandolier – a belt-like strap - of shells for the 12 gauge pump shotgun with the twenty inch barrel which sat snug in the pocket of the driver's door, ready for action.

By his side was his fourteen year old son Carl, a small wiry kid with a shock of reddish hair brushed upwards from his freckled face with its wide mouth and squarish chin. He wore a loose ragged shirt, baggy wide trousers and strong leather shoes. He also had an automatic pistol hanging from a belt somewhere under the loose shirt.

They both sat in the battered Land Rover listening intently

above the strong beat of the engine, listening for any sound as they searched the street for any warning of an imminent attack. The road was empty apart from a smouldering vehicle at the furthest end of the rubble strewn tarmac. The few remaining houses in the street, once called Belling Avenue, were in ruins, with many of the houses just burnt out skeletons of roof beams and tottering brick walls. Between the houses and in the streets surrounding the old Belling Avenue, what was once neatly kept gardens and pavements was now overgrown with weeds and grass and was the hunting grounds of feral cats, wild dogs and wolves.

The radio on the Defenders dashboard crackled into life; 'Hi, Dave... You copy?'

'Hello, Mister Richardson,' Carl said after snatching up the radio's mike, 'we've just left the house. Should be at the crossroads in about five minutes.'

'Oh, hi, Carl,' came the response, 'see you at the crossroads, then.' The radio went dead as the Defender moved forward with a muffled roar. It was always good thinking, when anyone wanted to go shopping, to go within a convoy, a line of trucks, however small, just in case of attack, as travelling in one vehicle was asking for trouble. They drove on slowly down the rubble-strewn road, turning left at the burnt out petrol station and on towards the high street and the crossroads. They purred along the old high street with its burnt out shops with their broken windows and smashed doors, relics of before, when it was a local shopping area.

As they approached the crossroads where an old abandoned single-deck red bus lay on its side with smashed windows and sagging tyres, and the broken traffic lights hung slanted across the road, they saw the old white Transit van of John Richardson growling its way towards them with its bolted on machine gun sticking out of the roof with Mrs Richardson with her hands on the grip, at the ready. The Richardson's were an older couple and by now should have been in comfortable retirement, but of necessity, had bravely fought on, although beneath Mrs Richardson's steel helmet, as she sat, finger on the trigger of the machine gun, her weathered face was lined, and her hair was grey.

With the Defender taking the lead, the little convoy of two vehicles left the houses behind and began the long run along the top of the grassy ridge to the shop in the distance. There was little chance of an attack on their way to the shop, it was after they had shopped and were on their way home that they would have to be careful, as they would be loaded with goods. So David cruised the Defender along the dusty road, followed by the Transit, only being watchful when they passed a clump of trees on a bend in the road in case there was an ambush.

'It must have been so different,' Carl muttered to his dad as he constantly visually swept the horizon outside of the Defender, 'before the Breakdown.'

'Oh, it sure was,' answered David, 'there were parks and open spaces, police to keep the peace, buses to go out on, doctors and nurses at the local hospital, cinemas and clubs...'

'And you could go out without protection?' Carl asked one more of his never ending questions he always asked his dad when the story of life before the Breakdown was talked about, 'that sounds so crazy now, to go out without a gun. What caused the Breakdown dad?'

'Well, son,' David re-told the story one more time to his son, a story he had told him many times before, 'prices for shopping and general living were rising for everyone and work and wages were not getting any better. Crime was on the rise all the time, but with the costs of living escalating on a daily basis, they reduced the number of police on the streets, and doctors and nurses, and security personnel; all these cutbacks were to cut community costs, but then the terrorist attacks on the citizens in the streets got worse.

'But I suppose the real bombshell was the manufacturing countries of Asia. They had a financial crises; you see the rest of the world had problems with corruption in Governments and tax avoidance, and so borrowed money to pay for goods from the manufacturing nations. Of course this could not go on and these countries had eventually to pay their bills, but to do so, they cut down more and more on social services, like hospitals and policing, and care in the community and so on. The countries grew poorer, and were not able to import goods. Then most Governments looked in on themselves and members of parliaments took what assets, like money and property that they could, to keep themselves rich and above the failing infrastructure holding the countries together.

'The workers, after the nation's bills had been settled, the very people who held things together, could not be paid, and went on strike, that is, they would not do their jobs until they were paid fairly for what they did. And the people on strike were the police, hospital workers, doctors, refuse collectors, transport people, like buses and trains, airport workers, docks where goods were brought into the country, immigration officials, everyone went on strike for good pay and living conditions. It was a country-wide general strike; everyone in the country was on strike, but they did not get anything, so they had no work and no money. The Governments of many countries collapsed, and warlords and gangs took over. And that's what we have now.

'What we're hoping for, all of us all the time, is that our Government will get back some sort of power and re-form into a new way of running the country and bringing back real law and order, it's been seven years now.

'Yeah, but we've got law and order,' said Carl, 'we've got The Force, they keep order...'

'Yes, I know, but Carl,' David said slowly and quietly, to emphasise his point, 'The Force is really just a big gang. The leader of The Force, Guy Treacher is a gang leader, a warlord. Look, the Richardson's behind us in their Transit van, they are bakers, with a bakery. The Force protect the Richardson's while they supply The Force with bread.

'I'm a gunsmith with my own little factory at the back of our house, The Force protects us and our family home because I supply them with guns. The folk who supply me with my materials are also protected by The Force. Anyone who stopped supplying The Force would not be protected any more and would soon be taken over or wiped out by gangs and other warlords, or even by The Force themselves if they wanted to. So they are not law and order, The Force is exactly what it's name says it is: A Force. They keep the peace by force, but only while it suits them. And if a bigger, more powerful gang than The Force comes along and fights them... well it all starts again.'

After a short while, the two vehicles arrived at the barbed wire grille which surrounded the shop. The shop, a big grey coloured warehouse building with two red stripes painted down the side, as all Force buildings and vehicles were painted to show their authority, was of course operated by The Force. At each corner of the barbed wire stood a tall wooden tower, where a machine gun toting Force man watched all around. At the gate to the shop, two grim-faced Force men checked all the vehicles going in and coming out of the compound. All the Force soldiers seemed to be alike, men and women, and they all had scruffy shirts, jeans and thick boots, and all carried weapons of one sort or another; rifles, hand guns or machine guns, and all carried long knives, swords or bayonets in their belts.

David and the Richardson's parked their vehicles in the allotted area inside the fencing, beside two armoured cars, both painted grey with the two stripes of The Force, where David and Carl collected a supermarket trolley and entered the warehouse, which was laid out inside exactly like a normal supermarket, but none of the items on the dusty, half filled shelves was priced. Inside, the warehouse was large, old and dirty, with lined avenues of shelves containing the goods for sale

All the food items on the shelves were canned and had old, faded and torn labels, although also on sale were tools, like hammers, saws, axes, drills and screwdrivers, and guns.

David and Carl picked up some of the food items that they needed and generally had a look around. 'Hey, dad,' Carl said, picking up a rusty toy car, 'what's this...?'

'Carl!' David grabbed Carl's hand and shook until the

toy was dropped back onto the shelf, 'don't just take anything from a shelf. You know that The Force has men patrolling inside the shop, if they even think you are stealing, they will gun you down without a second thought.'

'Ow! Of course, sorry dad,' Carl looked fearfully in each direction in case someone was going to point a gun at him. Luckily for him, there was no one around at that time. Carl felt his face go red as he drew away.

Father and son walked around the aisles collecting a few more of the canned goods that they wanted from the dusty shelves and went to the checkout. There was no till at the checkout, just a thin man sitting with a notepad and pen in his hands, a man with long black hair and a sneer on his unshaven chin who looked the customers over with narrowed eyes. Behind this man stood another member of The Force with a short machine pistol in his hand, ready for anyone who wanted to take a quick run out of the building, or argue over the asking barter price of an item.

The checkout man said in a bored voice as he viewed their trolley, 'Seven cans of grub, a bag of assorted screws, five metal drill bits and four large bottles of clean water,' he wrote all the items down carefully in his notepad, keeping a check on everything, 'you want any petrol?'

'Yes, we'll take four of the big containers,' David said, and then added, 'please.'

'You're Mortimer the gunsmith, right?' the checkout man said after squinting up at David.

'Yes, I am.' David agreed.

'OK, you're barter is good while you supply The Force,' intoned the man without looking up, 'you can go.' David and Carl took their goods to their vehicle, stashed their purchases then reversed the Defender onto a smaller hut which was at the side of the warehouse, where large containers of fuel were kept. Here they helped themselves to four of the petrol cans, watched over carefully by a Force member armed with a large sword. They loaded the cans onto their vehicle and drove out of the gates of the warehouse on their way home.

'You know, dad,' Carl said as they waited for the Richardson's Transit to appear behind them and then drove on, beyond the Force men on the gate of the barbed fence, into the open countryside, 'I notice that there's less and less on the shelves in the Force's warehouse, even the cans of petrol they sell, there seems to be less of everything.'

'Yes, I noticed that too,' David Answered, 'but of course, we are living in a "scavengers" society. We're still living on the left overs of Before; the goods still to be discovered in factories and store houses up and down the country. What will happen to us all, when the goods from Before dry up, I don't know. All we can hope for is that the Government re-forms and brings us back real law and order, and gets manufacturing and farming for animal feed and growing fruit and veg...'

The two vehicles headed out into the open countryside, leaving the barbed wire fence of the compound behind, as they rumbled along the dusty road. The tiny convoy headed out into the lonely countryside, rumbling along in the empty roads, heading homeward.

'Hey, heads up!' John Richardson's voice sprang from the radio speaker, 'I hear the buzz of motorbikes... and yeah, I can see them in my mirrors. We got company!' Both the homeward bound vehicles leapt forward as the drivers floored their accelerators. The buzz of bikes behind them meant only one thing. Bandits: gangs of young people on powerful motorbikes who murdered people and took from them their food, goods and guns, and then rode on.

David ripped up the microphone of his radio and roared into it: 'Hey! The Force men! It's David Mortimer! We've just been to the warehouse and we're headed home. We're being attacked by bikers! We need help!'

Then David saw as well, in his rear view mirror, the puff of smoke in the distance behind the Richardson's Transit as the bikers began to catch up. There were four bikes, and as they neared the fleeing motors, he could see the highly coloured painted faces of the riders and their passengers, young people wearing vests, shorts and boots, with flying hair, screaming and waving guns at the vehicles they chased.

David continued through the tree-lined countryside, faster and faster, trying to put as much distance between the riders as he could. Further and further they went as Mrs Richardson swivelled round and trained her machine gun on the advancing bikes. Ba-ba-ba-ba-ba-ba-bang her gun rang out as the bikers weaved from side to side behind them, as they fired back. Ting! Ting! Ting! The bullets from the biker's guns slammed into the metal of the Transit's bodywork.

David rounded a bend in the lane at breakneck speed only to slam on the brakes and come skidding to a halt in front of a large tree which was lying across the road. 'That wasn't here earlier,' breathed David, 'those bikers must've watched us go to the warehouse and moved it there to trap us on the way back.' Behind, Mrs Richardson still fired her gun, bringing down one of the bikes in a tumble of smoke and dust. The other three bikes roared on up to the now stopped motors, firing into them, one shot after another. Mrs Richardson dropped into the back of the van, whether she was shot or just dodging bullets was not clear.

Carl opened his window, dropped the wire mesh protecting the glass and fired his pistol at the approaching bikes, as the leading robber swerved and the passenger behind him fired a shotgun at the Defender. Bullets were whizzing through the air, bikes were skidding to a halt in the dust, metal was being hit with shells and glass was shattering. With a bump the Transit came to a stop, hitting the back of the Defender knocking David and Carl forward in their seats. When they shook their heads and looked up again, they were looking down the barrels of five assorted guns as the bikers stood in front of David's driver's door. One of the biker's had slid off his bike and gone to capture the Richardson's from their van.

The biker raiders were all teenagers or in their early twenties, with their faces glowing in bright multi-coloured paints, with their sloppy vests, baggy shorts and long boots. All had ammunition-filled gun belts with pistol holsters at their sides or shotguns or rifles in their hands. Many of these young people had scratches, bruises or deep body or facial scars from previous battles.

'Hey. You, boy,' one of the raiders, a tall young man with intense eyes and a sneer on his curled lips said, 'put your gun down. If you even raise that weapon now, we'll kill your old man.' Some of the gun barrels turned to point directly at David. Carl pulled his hand away from his now holstered pistol.

'Now all of you, get out of your vehicle,' instructed the young man, 'lay your weapons on the ground and start walking. We'll let you go. We'll have your vehicles and your grub, but you can go.' The bikers stood back, grinning.

'Dad!' Carl whispered, 'let's get going...'

'Don't run, Carl,' David said from the corner of his mouth, 'it's just what they want. As soon as you run, they'll hunt you down and kill you. It will be some sport for them. Just do everything slowly, let me take the first hit at them, then fight for your life.' David and Carl very slowly moved for the door handles of the car, turning them gently.

'Come on!' shouted the leader of the bikers as David saw the Richardson's being dragged from their van. As the vicious biker bullied and prodded the old couple along with the butt of his rifle, David saw how old and defenceless the couple were, but he could do nothing about it. They were pushed down to the ground in front of the line of raiders. The leader of the bikers got angry and shouted: 'Get on with...' Boom! a shot rang out as the leader's face turned bright red and his head exploded as a single bullet ripped through his brain. Boom! Boom! two more bikers burst into blood-sprouting bodies as they fell to the ground. The rest of the robbers dropped to the ground but were picked off by the deadly sniper fire of a distant assassin in a short series of barking single shots, one after the other. Soon all were dead, as one after the other of the bikers fell to a single shot.

'Look there!' Carl pointed along the ground into a nearby field where a vehicle, painted grey with the two red stripes of

The Force had been parked. A single marksman, leaning across the bonnet of the car with a sniper rifle had killed all the raiders. By the gunman's side stood another Force soldier, with binoculars held to his eyes, watching the action.

Later that night, when the two vehicles had made it back to their homes and they were safely barricaded in, Carl told his mum of the raid by the bikers on their journey home. '...and we were saved, mum, saved by the Force...'

'Yes, but you must remember, Carl,' David informed his son, 'The Force only looks after us because we supply them with what they want, same as the Richardson's. If they didn't need us, they'd have let us die. If ever the Government gets back, you will see the real meaning of good law and order.'

'Well, at least they kept you safe,' said mum, sweeping back her brown hair over her tanned face, 'maybe one day you'll see the police and the military get back in governmental power with a new countrywide, stable governorship. But for now it was The Force that looked after us.'

Time passed and David and Carl went to work, as usual in the workshop of their gunsmith's, manufacturing by hand many handguns and rifles, storing them away for when The Force next sent their men for "the reckoning" when the family had to pay for its freedom and protection with the goods they had made.

Then one day, Carl noticed something in the sky; a plume of black smoke drifting high into the clouds. 'It's strange,' David said when Carl pointed it out, 'the smoke cloud seems to be hovering over the warehouse of The Force.' Then came great booms and bangs of explosions, followed by the distant sound of machine gun fire and vehicle's racing by, near to their own compound. The family stayed indoors, too afraid to go out and get involved in whatever it was that was happening outside. They kept well within their own back yard of the workshop.

Days later, Carl was out in the yard moving some empty petrol cans when he heard it. He looked up into the sky and stopped what he was doing with a shout. 'Dad! Dad! Come and look at this! I've never seen one of these before!' David ran out into the yard and saw what it was that had his son so taken by surprise.

It was an airplane! Clattering along in the sky was an ancient bi-plane. It had two sets of wings, one above the other, and a long fuselage leading to a high tail. It was all held together by wires and the body of the plane was made of fabric. At the front a large wooden propeller spun pulling the ancient airplane along in the sky. A man in the front of the plane, the pilot, looked down at the men in the yard. He held a rifle in his hand and waved at them.

'It must be what you've always wanted!' Carl shouted above the noise to his father as his mum joined them, looking up at the flying machine, 'it must be the Government, who have defeated The Force and are taking over the country again.'

'No, no it's not,' David sighed, 'I know you've never seen an airplane before Carl, but a real government airplane would not be that old crate, with a guy leaning out waving a rifle. I reckon that this is the other thing that we knew could happen. It's another warlord and his gang, just like The Force. And the smoke was the battle they have had for ownership of this territory. We must now be in the protection of another warlord, and who says how they will treat us?'

Better the devil you know

It is often better to deal with someone or something you are familiar with and know, even if they are not ideal.

If you are enoying reading this book of short stories, have you read Terry's other book of short tales *BYTES*

Another good read is *DOORS*.

This is the story of a medieval warrior who watches his wife disappear into a time warp, then follows her to bring her back. These adventures are chronicled as he travels around history seeking his spouse

GOOD LUCK – BAD LUCK

James "Jimmy" Boswell's eyes opened slowly. He blinked a few times at the sunlight streaming through the half closed curtains, then looked around the room with a sick feeling as he surveyed his "apartment" which was on the top floor of an old house. His room; it reminded Jimmy of his achievements in life. The dirty and sad wallpaper was torn and hanging off in some places, and the tiny TV - still on from last night - sitting perched on the end of his white chest of drawers, which had black marks over it around the sagging drawer handles. The carpet was threadbare and in the corner sat a stool with an old cream coloured microwave oven standing on it, his only way of home cooking. Along by the other wall of his room, on the floor amid some empty beer bottles, lay his outdoor clothes of rumpled T-shirt, old floppy cardigan, scruffy blue jeans and ancient white trainers with black scuff marks.

Jimmy lifted himself up in the cot bed and chucked off his dark blue blanket. He was still in his vest and pants from yesterday, after he had come home late last night and thrown himself straight into his bed.

He staggered up and stood in front of the mirror which hung lop-sidedly from the wall. He looked at himself in disgust, as he scratched his head at his reflection. He was twenty-seven years old, losing his hair and had a floppy belly and fat legs. His vacant brown eyes stared back at him through the misty mirror, at his pink and white skin, his stubby nose and wet lips which were open in a half surprised gawp on his unshaven chin.

As he pulled on his clothes, those that he had worn yesterday, including the smelly trainers, he pondered his bleak future. He hadn't had a job for two months since he had lost his enjoyable employment in the jewellers shop, where he had been happy to work, and had a future to look forward to. But when the shop had closed he had become unemployed, lost his way a bit and was now stony broke, but he had been working for

Kenny, an old school mate, down at Kenny's Car Wash, outside the council flats off the high street. Kenny hadn't paid him for his work yet, as he needed cash to pay the rent for his business, but was going to pay Jimmy today.

So to see him through, Jimmy had had a loan of fifty quid from big Andrei, who hung out with his mates in a betting shop near the Docklands Light Railway station. That fifty quid loan had been quickly spent, in the sure knowledge that Jimmy would be paid today. And today was also pay back time to big Andrei, which was OK except for the fact that Kenny had done a runner. Gone missing. Disappeared.

What was that? A tap tap down below him, on the window of the front door of the house. Jimmy froze: could it be big Andrei? Could the burly European be knocking at the door for the return of his fifty quid from Jimmy? 'Wait! Don't panic,' he thought, 'this old house is divided into many "flats" - single rooms, really - where everyone shares the bathroom, kitchen and loo. The tap tap could be for any one of the other residents.' Jimmy waited, and as he waited, he slid up to the window and pulled the old curtain to one side so that he could see outside. He couldn't make out who was at the front door, but it looked bad; no one had answered the front door yet, not a peep from any of the other residents.

The rising tension was too much, as the whole house went eerily quiet. Jimmy trod from his room down the rickety stairs in a doomed daze, he would throw himself onto the mercy of big Andrei and hope to be given time to pay - after he got a quick slap from Andrei of course - but Jimmy just couldn't stand the suspense of not knowing. He arrived at the bottom of the stairs, stepped forward and opened the front door.

'Andrei, look...' he blurted, then stopped dead in his tracks, 'Alf! What you doin' here? You've been missing for what... six weeks?' The young man who had been tapping on the door was, to say the least, frail. He was extremely thin, gaunt and gangly and his blond hair was loose and stringy, hanging over his eyes and ears. His deeply set grey eyes were almost covered in droopy eyelids, and his long nose was slightly wet over a thick lipped mouth showing a large black gap in the middle of a set of long teeth. Alf was wearing a button up cardigan with sleeves which covered his hands and wore old black trousers which were shiny and on his narrow feet were ancient brown boots.

'Yeah, well,' Alf began his explanation in a hollow sounding voice, 'See... I sort of levered open the side window of a shop in the high street to see if there was anything inside worth taking, then when I left the shop, some old dame said she thought she recognised me getting out of the window, so I thought I should disappear for a while, so when the Old Bill finally do catch me, the ancient granny's memory will have faded a bit and she might have forgot me. I visited me uncle in Bognor for a while.'

'But when I last saw you,' Jimmy said with urgency in his voice, 'you took that old Rock 'n' Roll guitar I had inherited from my aunty, and were taking it to the pawnbrokers to sell for me. What happened?'

'Well...' Alf stammered, 'I got to the pawnbroker's shop alright, but it was as I came out of the shop that the old girl said she recognised me. So I had to run...'

'So how much did you get for my guitar.' Jimmy demanded, and where's my money, now?'

'I got a hundred quid for the guitar, it was a quality instrument,' Alf said with a quiver in his tone, 'but I borrowed some of the cash for the trip to Bognor... but I got the rest of the dough here for you.'

'How much have your got for me, then?' Jimmy was almost too afraid to ask.

'Here,' Alf thrust a soggy banknote into Jimmy's hand and ran from the doorstep, crying out as he went: 'I'll pay you back one day Jimmy, honest!'

Jimmy opened the crumpled banknote and smiled a wide smile when he saw that it was a fifty pound note, 'No, you won't pay me back one day, Alf,' he muttered almost to himself, 'but you have probably just saved my life.' He carefully folded the worn fifty quid note and put it in his cardigan pocket. Now he could pay back big Andrei and not get beaten to a pulp.

Jimmy pulled up the zip on his baggy cardigan, stepped out and slammed the front door behind him. There was no time to lose, he would go to big Andrei, pay him the fifty pound note as soon as possible; only then would he feel free, and not fear being set upon by Andrei or his bully boys.

He marched down to his local Docklands Light Railway station and joined in with the crowds pushing, bumping and surging forward into the station. 'What are all these people doing here?' he thought as he struggled along in their midst to sneak onto the platform without first buying a ticket. 'Of course!' he laughed to himself as the train rumbled into the station and the whole surging crowd tried to get on board at the same time, 'it's the rush hour!' he muttered to himself, 'I've never seen so many people on the trains. Of course, they're all going to work! When I worked at the jeweller's shop, I had to get in early to open up, so I missed the rush hour.'

As the main crowd pushed and shoved into the carriage, Jimmy kept himself near the doors as he was only going one stop. He stood just holding himself away from an old girl who was daydreaming as she peered out of the window of the carriage door. Jimmy stood still in the crowded train and waited for the one stop to the next station and to big Andrei. A young man stood close to Jimmy, he was almost pressed between Jimmy and the door, and Jimmy took a quick peek at him. The guy was in his twenties, had dark hair shaved close to his scalp, brown eyes, a sharp nose on his dusky skinned face with a thin moustache and beard. He wore a black round necked T-shirt under a brown three-quarter length coat and dark blue jeans and black trainers. Instinctively, Jimmy slid away from the guy.

The train suddenly skidded to a halt, making half of the passengers fall forward. When the doors opened, Jimmy slid easily in with the mass of bodies and let himself be swept to the barrier where he walked purposefully to one side and down to a quieter end of the row of ticket machines. Here he vaulted over the barrier and walked smartly away without looking back. If a passenger was watching him, they did not cry out or report his behaviour to anyone. Jimmy walked on.

At the exit of the station where the people separated and went their different ways, Jimmy marched off briskly to the betting shop and a first ever easy meeting with big Andrei; he'd pay off the man and never see him again. Then he'd get a new job and start living again.

Just as Jimmy entered the betting shop, he saw a gaggle of men over in the corner and knew that was where big Andrei would be. Jimmy felt in his cardigan pocket for one last reassuring touch of the fifty pound note. 'Oh,' he thought, 'not in that pocket. Must be in the other one.' Jimmy searched the other pocket of the cardigan. He stopped in mid stride, just as he was half way in the shop doorway. Both pockets were empty! How could that be? Panic! He turned and fled. Was that big Andrei? Did the huge man just look up from the crowd and look directly at Jimmy? Or was he mistaken? Jimmy ran out of the shop and into the street.

His head was in a spin. What could have happened to his life-saving fifty pound note? Oh, no! The truth hit him like a brick landing on his head. That guy! The one on the train, the one who had stood near to him. Jimmy *knew* there had been something about him. He had been a pickpocket. Jimmy's pocket had been dipped. And dipped by a professional. Jimmy wandered aimlessly on. What was he going to do?

The hours passed by quickly as the day moved on, and with it, the expected life span of Jimmy as well, as he walked the busy city streets. He ambled on and on, not looking into the faces of the people who brushed by him, scampering along on their busy day, their thoughts on other things. His only thoughts were himself: Jimmy, eyes downcast, knowing that he had to see Andrei before the end of the day or he would be on Andrei's "find" list – not a place to be if you liked good health.

'Oof!' Jimmy went sprawling backwards onto the

pavement. Rolling over and sitting up, he squinted along the pavement, expecting the worse, the worse that is, in the expectation that Andrei or friends had found him. When he got up the courage to actually fully open his eyes he was surprised to see who had knocked him over and was now on the ground with him.

A solidly-built woman had bumped into him, bowling him right over. She had frizzy dark brown hair, bright brown eyes in her brown skinned face with bright red lip-sticked mouth and white teeth. She wore a bright red frilly long sleeved blouse and tight black leggings with shiny red shoes with tall, spiky heels. The shopping bags she had been carrying were now laying on the ground by her side spilling their contents over the pavement.

'Aw, sorry, fella!' she said in a London-Caribbean accent as she struggled up, 'I wos jus' tuckin' a card into me phone, not lookin' where I was goin' an' wham! Here we are.' Jimmy scrambled up, helped put her goods back into her bags, straightened himself up, and dusted himself down, and the mystery woman strode off and disappeared into the crowd, hurrying along.

'Wow,' Jimmy said to himself as the crowd on the busy pavement closed in behind her. As he turned to continue his aimless walking, he looked down onto the pavement, and then he saw it. A scruffy, torn and worn mobile phone cover, obviously missed when picking up the young lady's spilled shopping. Jimmy picked it up, knowing all the while that her phone would be inside the cover. He flicked it open and sure enough the phone was in there.

He decided almost immediately: he'd walk into a shop and hand the phone over to a member of staff and say he'd found the phone on the floor in their shop, then the shop people would phone her and tell her that they had her mobile and she could pick it up, that way it'd no longer be his problem. Then he noticed the top of a small card sticking out from the inside of the phone. 'Oh, yeah,' Jimmy said to himself as he stood on the pavement, the passers-by bustling around him, the buzzing traffic whizzing by on the road, 'she said she was tucking a card into her phone, not looking where she was going.'

Jimmy pulled out the card, it was a scratch card, one of those that you could get in many shops and supermarkets. He turned it towards him, 'it's showing three 50's; what's the prize for three 50's I wonder?' He stared in disbelief at the prize printed on the scratched-out surface of the card. It was £50!!!

Jimmy couldn't believe it! Fifty quid! His life was saved *again*! How his luck had changed! Jimmy once more made a plan; he would hand the "lost" phone in to a shop, as was his initial plan, but, instead of the winning scratch card inside, he would leave a small message explaining that he had made a note of her telephone number and would repay the fifty quid as soon as he could but needed it right now for an emergency. Then he'd get the prize of fifty smackers and run to Andrei's betting shop headquarters before the day was out and save his life!

Jimmy was so pleased! He felt the soft glow of pleasure in the knowledge that he would not be beaten into a sticky mess by Andrei and his crew today. So happy was he that he didn't notice the swirling crowds around him nor the buzz of the powerful little motor scooter as it raced down the inside of the suddenly almost grid-locked traffic on the packed city street. All Jimmy saw was the flash of the black and white scooter, the black clad rider and passenger, the red and white of the pair's crash helmets and the smack on his hand as the passenger snatched the phone out of Jimmy's hand.

'Thanks sunshine!' cried the passenger on the back of the bike as it whisked by in a fraction of a second, 'you just been done by the Sunshine Gang!' The bike sped off, weaving in and out of the queueing cars, buses and vans. Jimmy was left speechless. He just looked open mouthed at his empty hand as the bike sped round the nearest corner, and was gone.

In a complete dazed state of shock, Jimmy looked around him on the pavement. People were just carrying on, marching along on the busy pavement, unaware of what had just happened. It had all been so quick, all over in a few seconds. Jimmy staggered on in a dream-like haze.

Jimmy wandered on in his fuzzy mental state, aimlessly thinking of the horrible day he was having, then he noticed; was it turning slightly dark? Was the afternoon closing down into the end of the day? If he didn't get to Andrei's... He made just one more plan, one of desperation. He would walk back to Andrei's and throw himself on the big man's mercy and hope for another day to find the fifty pounds... but deep in the back of his mind, he knew that he didn't have much of a chance, Andrei would not let anyone get away with anything, as it might damage his reputation.

But he could think of no other option. He turned and began the long walk back to the dreaded betting shop, a long and lonely walk. He trudged along the streets, oblivious of his surroundings, just thinking about his return meeting to come with big Andrei and his boys.

As he turned a corner on his return to the betting shop, a small, grey haired man turned and locked a shop door with a hefty gold coloured key. The shop's window, by the side of the door was full of "Opening Soon" posters. The man walked over to the kerbside and looked this way and that, possibly looking for a taxi. He was an older man with shrewd brown eyes, a ruddy complexion, smooth shaven chin and a white moustache. He wore a red tie on his white shirt and a dark brown suit with brown shoes, and he carried a black brief case.

This time Jimmy did hear the muffled roar of the scooter as it roared alongside the pavement passed the busy queueing cars in the road. He saw the flash of the black and white scooter's body panels, the black clad rider and passenger, and the red and white of the men's crash helmets and the thwack as the passenger snatched the brief case out of the man's hand.

'Thanks sunshine!' cried the bike's passenger as it zoomed by at speed, 'you just been done by the Sunshine Gang!'

'Not this time!' Jimmy shouted as he threw himself at the speeding bike as it passed him. Thump! He barrelled into the escaping pair. The bike was pushed violently over to one side and without even slowing down smashed into the back of an open-backed truck, throwing rider and passenger onto the tarmac, where they rolled over and over.

The truck driver stopped and ran around his vehicle to see what had run into his vehicle. Passers-by had seen the veering bike and also came into the road. Traffic stopped: a police car arrived. Rider and passenger where not badly hurt but held onto by the public for the police to take. Jimmy pulled the brief case from the thieving bikers and grabbed the phone from the biker passenger's pocket that was stolen from him earlier. Then Jimmy handed the briefcase back to the grey haired man.

In the midst of the chaos an ambulance arrived, while the man who had had his brief case stolen explained to the police what had happened to him. The ambulance later left with the bikers and two policemen, who were to take the prisoners to the police station after they had been seen by the doctors at the hospital.

As other police directed the traffic and moved the thieves' bike to the side of the road, the briefcase man approached Jimmy. 'Well, young man,' he said with a smile, 'I'm very glad you stopped those two. I'm opening a new shop here, and this briefcase holds some rather expensive samples of jewellery. So I must reward you in some way...'

'No, look, it's alright,' Jimmy was even more conscious of the fading light of the afternoon, and the thought of Andrei's annoyance if he were late, 'no, I've got to go.'

'Look, old chap,' continued the briefcase man, 'I must reward you in some way for what you have done today.' The man pulled a wallet from his inside pocket and took out a banknote, pressing it firmly into Jimmy's hand. 'And if ever you're looking for a job, well, I'm opening a new shop here and I saw you are brave and honest. If you think you could work in a jeweller's shop...'

'Jeweller's shop!' Jimmy cried, 'but that's what I was doing before I lost my last job. The shop owner moved away and I was left redundant...'

'That's settled then,' smiled the man, 'come and see me at the shop tomorrow, and start working for me.' The two shook hands, as Jimmy turned to go, he had to see Andrei soon.

That was when he looked down at his hand and saw what the man had pressed onto his palm. A £50 note! He had had some unbelievable luck this day. He started to march off to see Andrei, then on impulse turned back to the policemen who were clearing up the dropped debris from the bikers. 'Oh, by the way,' he said to one of the coppers, 'I found this mobile phone on the street, someone must have lost it in the confusion.' He dropped the phone with its winning scratch card inside into the policeman's hand and, clutching hard onto the £50 pound note in his hand, went on to clear his debt with Andrei.

To beggar belief

Anything that seems so strange as to be unbelievable.

BANDIDO'S

'Here we are, Shreya,' Charlie Durnsford smiled to his girlfriend sitting in the passenger seat, as he saw the roadside shack at the side of the dusty traffic-free road, 'here's somewhere to get a coffee, or a cold drink.' They rumbled to a stop in their bright red coloured hired Jeep, followed by a cloud of dust, as the fierce sun shone down with a heavy intensity. As the Jeep stopped, they saw the battered and slightly lopsided sign which read: *CANTINA*. All around them was open countryside, with huge mountains in the distance over the desert-like terrain, with sandy ground and cactus-like trees and bushes.

The two looked gratefully at the tiny wooden shack on the lonely Mexican road, out in the middle of the hot, humid, empty, countryside. They were both in their middle twenties; Charlie was short and slim, with his dark brown hair cut short at the sides and he sported a thin beard and moustache on his pale skinned face. Thin dark eyebrows over brown eyes and a narrow nose showed above a thin mouth giving a slightly one-sided grin. He wore an old red polo shirt, worn blue jeans and soft suede shoes.

Shreya Wadeyla was slightly taller than Charlie and was darker skinned, with black hair, sparkling dark eyes, short nose and wide mouth. She wore a white blouse, dark red shorts, and flat black slip-on shoes.

This would be the last of their holiday adventures, to fly half way round the world from England just to look at the countryside on another continent, after which they intended to settle down and pursue their careers at home for a financially secure future. They got out of the Jeep and stepped into the blistering heat of the day, and hurried towards the shade of the cantina.

The small clapboard-built cantina was old, it had red tiles on its slanted roof and its wooden walls were cracked with the daily heat of the Mexican Matorral shrublands, a vast empty area of grass and bushes. A few unused old wooden chairs waited outside the cantina sitting in the glaring sun. Charlie and Shreya walked quickly passed them into the bar.

Inside, the bar was not cool, but it at least had shade, and its tiny interior walls were hung with old photographs showing cowboy types on horseback, swirling ropes or lassoing cattle in the clouds of dust on a ranch. There were no other customers.

There were a few round tables with chairs placed around them on the dusty floor and at one end of the old cabin was a flat topped wooden counter, behind which was a shelf with a long line of bottles of some spirits or other while in a corner was a humming cola vending machine. Sitting behind the bar and smoking a small cigar was a short man with black straggly hair, dark eyebrows and deep set dark eyes, he had a droopy black moustache and lots of stubbly beard on his small, lined face. He wore an old checked shirt, tattered blue jeans and tall cowboy boots.

'Hi, my tourist friends,' he said in broken English, 'what refreshing drink can I get for you today? Or would you like to stay for eats?' From a small open door behind the man came the exotic smells of spicy cooking. Without saying any more, Shreya and Charlie made for the vending machine and bought a cold drink. Soon the pair were drinking down the icy cold fizzy liquid.

'Wow, that's great smelling food,' Charlie said with interest, 'what is it?'

'My wife, she makes the best food,' said the cantina man, 'we have Nachos covered with melted cheese, turkey Fajitas, king prawn Taco's, corn tortillas and Enchiladas...'

'Ooh! That sounds great,' Charlie could taste it already, 'oh yeah, let's stop for a meal while we're here,'

'Sure thing boss,' the man jumped from his seat and ducked into the back room, quickly emerging with two menus. 'Here, my friends,' he said throwing the menus onto a nearby table, 'take your time and make your choice, after all, it's fifty miles to the nearest town, you might as well eat now. You don't want to stop on this road any more today. You never know, bandits are still around in this part of the country.'

The two sat and studied the menus, 'You don't think there really are bandits up in the hills,' Shreya asked, suddenly looking up, 'do you, Charlie?'

'Of course not,' Charlie laughed, 'that's just to make it sound exciting for the tourists. I reckon maybe one hundred years ago it would have been unsafe to travel on your own, because of highwaymen and bandits, but we're not in the nineteenth century now.' They made their choices for their meal, and were soon delving into the piled up plates of food which came from the tantalizing smells of the kitchen.

Two hours later, the two paid their bill for their meal and left, and they climbed happily into their vehicle and drove off. 'That was a lovely meal, I'm absolutely full,' Shreya said, 'and we don't want to stop again on this road if there really is a danger of being stopped by bandits.'

'Oh, I don't think there's much danger of that,' Charlie laughed, 'I think bandits on horseback may be a bit out of date by now.' They drove on.

They motored on along the one and only road into the deep countryside, the green grass and brush sometimes changing into desert-like sand and tumbleweed blowing in the hot breeze, the Sat-Nav now quiet as they followed the single winding road into the hot, sun drenched day. 'Wow, that was a great meal,' yawned Charlie, 'could'ave done with a longer stay.'

'Yes,' agreed Shreya, 'I'm still full up.' She leaned back into her seat, opened the window slightly and closed her eyes. Charlie shook his head to clear the drowsiness he was feeling and concentrated on keeping the jeep on the winding dirt road.

The miles rumbled passed under the wheels of their vehicle, as the motor hummed gently and Charlie's eyes slowly closed. 'Ooh!' he jerked up, shook his head and dragged his eyes open, twisting the steering wheel over to keep him on the road. Charlie blinked, shook his head again and turned off the air conditioning, then pressed the button to open his drivers door window. The air that came billowing in from the heat outside made him feel hotter but its swirling motion forced him to keep awake.

Ten minutes later and Charlie once again jerked his head up and grabbed at the wheel to take them back onto the dusty road. That time they had completely left the road and were driving on grass! 'Gotta stop.' Charlie said out loud as he pulled up on the grass verge and looked at Shreya, who was completely out, sleeping like a babe. 'Just got to have five minutes.' Charlie switched off the engine and closed his eyes...

'Ouch!' Something had cracked into Charlie's cheek. He opened his eyes wide in shock as he tore himself awake. He then jumped even higher when he saw what it was that had hit him. It was a bony, gnarled fist. It belonged to a small man who was sitting in the saddle on a white horse and reaching into the open window of the Jeep, and who stared at him with wild, crazy eyes.

Reaching into the vehicle had pushed back a massive black sombrero hat from the man's head but it was now hanging down his back from his head by a cord round his throat. The man had black stringy hair which flopped round his face and head, and his dark sun-yellowed skin was lined and dirty. He had black eyebrows which knitted together over his black eyes and large nose and a twisted mouth, and his face was unshaven and sweaty. He wore a collar-less grey shirt with long sleeves which hung in tatters; a leather waistcoat and ancient blue jeans which were tucked into high black riding boots. Unbelievably, around the man's waist was a low slung belt upon which was a holstered six-shooter pistol.

'Hey! Hey! Compadre!' The man shouted into Charlie's face as he grabbed Charlie's shirt collar and twisted, 'what you doin' here on my land? Who are you? What you doin' here on my land? What's your name?'

'My name is Charlie...' blurted Charlie from his half

strangled throat, 'and I'm here on holiday... I mean vacation.'

'Well, me and my boys, we don't like it,' snarled the man through clenched teeth.

"Me and my boys"? Charlie thought as he looked beyond the crazy man. What he then saw was even more of a shock. Horses! There were at least ten of them, of many different colours. The horses all had riders in their saddles, who were dressed much like Charlie's attacker, all had pistol holsters on their belts and some even carried rifles, and they rode in a circle around the Jeep, pulling at the horses reins and jeered and laughed at Charlie.

'You is talking to Don Pedro Alvarez,' sneered the little man, tightening his grip on Charlie's shirt collar, 'I'm the big boss round here, number one bandit and Grand Theft Auto champion.'

'What...? What did you just say?' Charlie was confused, 'surely you're not bandits? I mean... that's a thing of the past, isn't it? Charlie looked innocently at the sweaty and furious man who tightly gripped his collar.

'Why you...' The little man became even more furious as his men began to shout and fire their guns into the air. Boom! Boom! The noise made Charlie jump each time. 'Of course, we're bandits,' cried the little man, 'but now we've got Sat Nav and computers... And what's this? Hey boys! Why, there's a pretty little girl in the car as well.'

A thick-set, powerful looking rider wearing an enormous round sombrero hat and an open grey coloured shirt and leather trousers trotted his horse over to the other side of the car and twisted the door handle, jerking the door open with a bang. His fat, sweaty face with thick stubble on its round chin peering into the car. He grabbed the slowly awakening Shreya from her seat, wrapping a large hand over her mouth to stifle her screams as she fully awoke to find herself being attacked. He dragged her from the car and pulled her onto the horse in front of him, laying her over the saddle. 'Hey! What're you doing?' Charlie shouted, as he tried to get his drivers door open, bashing it against the iron grip of Don Pedro Alvarez's fist.

'What's the matter,Charlie?' Alvarez shouted back, his frenzied eyes glaring back, Charlie! Charlie! Charlie!' The grip on Charlie's neck tightened even more, his head being shaken back and forth, as Charlie's eyes closed as he lost consciousness.

'Charlie! Charlie!' the voice echoed round and round in Charlie's head, as he slowly opened his eyes. 'Charlie! Charlie!' He looked, but the fierce look of Alvarez's eyes were replaced by the sparkling dark eyes of Shreya's as she shook him awake. 'Good job you stopped at the side of the road,' Shreya continued, 'that meal we had at the Cantina was a bit strong for us, I think. We both had to stop and have a doze, didn't we?'

Charlie looked out over the empty afternoon grassland of the surrounding countryside, and sighed gratefully: 'Oh, it was all a dream, then?'

'Yes, it must have been,' smiled Shreya, 'too much cheese in our meal, I reckon.'

You are what you eat

"A man is what he eats"

I hope that you have enjoyed my latest short story compliation. I tried to find a suitable parable to each of the tales but as you may know, and please check on line, there are hundreds of parable, moral stories and fables.
You may find one that suit a narrative better.
I have finished The Time Police Four, and I'm working on a follow up to the book Doors, which will be Doors 2.

Terry Howard   August 2018

Terry's other novels and where to find them
Hewitt's War
The Flying Four
Matthew's Schooldays
Mirror to the Past
The Time Police
The Time Police 2 - *Invasion*
The Time Police 3 - *Draco Returns*
Bytes
Doors

all of which have been published by
Amazon as paperback
and as Kindle versions

Follow Terry on Twitter@terryhoward21
also at
www.terryhowardauthor.wordpress.com/blog

CPSIA information can be obtained
at www.ICGtesting.com
Printed in the USA
BVHW041839290322
632767BV00013B/365

9 781729 821541